经典与创新
世界文学背景下中西比较诗学研究
THE CLASSIC AND CREATIVITY
A STUDY IN CHINESE AND WESTERN COMPARATIVE POETICS
IN THE AGE OF WORLD LITERATURE

蒋竹雨　著

上海外语教育出版社
外教社　SHANGHAI FOREIGN LANGUAGE EDUCATION PRESS

图书在版编目（CIP）数据

经典与创新：世界文学背景下中西比较诗学研究 /
蒋竹雨著 . -- 上海：上海外语教育出版社，2023
（外教社博学文库）
ISBN 978-7-5446-7886-5

Ⅰ.①经… Ⅱ.①蒋… Ⅲ.①诗学－比较研究－中国
、西方国家 Ⅳ.①I207.2 ②I106.2

中国国家版本馆 CIP 数据核字 (2023) 第 169585 号

出版发行：**上海外语教育出版社**
（上海外国语大学内） 邮编：200083
电　　话：021–65425300 (总机)
电子邮箱：bookinfo@sflep.com.cn
网　　址：http://www.sflep.com
责任编辑：苗　杨

印　　刷：上海叶大印务发展有限公司
开　　本：890×1240　1/32　印张 5.375　字数 182 千字
版　　次：2023 年 11 月第 1 版　 2023 年 11 月第 1 次印刷

书　　号：**ISBN 978-7-5446-7886-5**
定　　价：**30.00 元**

本版图书如有印装质量问题，可向本社调换
质量服务热线：4008-213-263

The Classic and Creativity: A Study in Chinese and Western Comparative Poetics in the Age of World Literature

博学文库
编委会成员

出版说明

　　上海外语教育出版社始终坚持"服务外语教育、传播先进文化、推广学术成果、促进人才培养"的经营理念，凭借自身的专业优势和创新精神，多年来已推出各类学术图书600余种，为中国的外语教学和研究作出了积极的贡献。

　　为展示学术研究的最新动态和成果，并为广大优秀的博士人才提供广阔的学术交流的平台，上海外语教育出版社隆重推出"外教社博学文库"。该文库遴选国内的优秀博士论文，遵循严格的"专家推荐、匿名评审、好中选优"的筛选流程，内容涵盖语言学、文学、翻译和教学法研究等各个领域。该文库为开放系列，理论创新性强、材料科学翔实、论述周密严谨、文字简洁流畅，其问世必将为国内外广大读者在相关的外语学习和研究领域提供又一宝贵的学术资源。

Foreword

The classic, like canon, is a term sometimes heatedly debated in contemporary literary criticism. They both refer to the best and the most significant literary works that serve as the standard and model of literary creation in a particular literary and cultural tradition. The classic or canonical works have pedagogical values for the education of the young, and they embody and cultivate the aesthetic taste and moral principles of the society as a whole for generations. Unlike the religious canon, the literary canon is changeable. Some classic works may lose their value and prestige as time moves on and the social circumstances change, while some other previously neglected works may rise to acquire the status of canonicity when their values are recognized and appreciated in a different social and historical condition. Exemplary works by talented female writers, for example, or canonical works in "minor" languages or from non-Western traditions are increasingly gaining visibility and reputation in our time and enriching our reading experience of great literature. World literature in particular offers a great opportunity today for the expansion of our horizon and for making more great works to become part of the canon of world literature.

The idea of the classic faces extraordinary challenges, but also great opportunities, with the rise of world literature, which enables and encourages us to access the best of literary works from different cultures and languages. By and large, however, canonical works discussed in world literature studies today still remain mostly Western, while canonical works in non-Western or even "minor" European literatures are still unknown and unrecognized. This is what I have called the yet-unknown world literature, and how to expand the world literary canon to include those unknown canonical works from the other traditions is still a major task for literary scholars, particularly scholars of comparative and world literature.

In contemporary criticism, there are ideological challenges to the idea of canon or the classic, and such challenges try to minimize the importance of the classic from politically and ideologically charged positions and to reduce the value of the classics as if they could be dismissed as merely clichés and the passé. Canon, however, is not made overnight by any political or ideological forces and it cannot be "decanonized" overnight, either. As vehicles of important cultural values and embodiments of aesthetic values of a particular tradition, canonical works of a literature will always be relevant to readers of different generations under very different social, historical, and political conditions. The classic, in other words, is always important and worthy of serious study and meticulous scholarship.

The literary classic is also always open to different understanding and interpretations. In fact, one indication of the vitality and continuous relevance of the classic is its ability to engage a variety of different critical approaches and interpretations. In the current book, Dr. Jiang observantly presents the emerging new ways to read, study and circulate literary classics in the present time, which will help literary scholars to cope with the challenges to the classics today without denigrating the significance of critical inquiries and investigations from various theoretical perspectives. This book will be of interest not only to university faculties who may encounter challenging questions about literary classics in their teaching, but also to literary scholars who are engaged in innovative studies of literary classics, and even to administrators in institutes of higher education who need to make decisions about how to use the classics to construct the basis of disciplinary and interdisciplinary studies in the humanities. I am confident that readers of different kinds will be able to find in this book something useful, interesting and beneficial, and will always gain something from their reading experience.

张隆溪

Zhang Longxi
Chair Professor of Comparative Literature and Translation
City University of Hong Kong
Foreign Member
The Royal Swedish Academy of Letters, History and Antiquities
Academia Europaea

前言

　　2011年的夏天，在完成了清华四年的本科学业后，我来到了香港城市大学，跟随张隆溪教授开始了为期四年的直博项目的学习。彼时的我对于即将开启的研究生活充满期待。清华四年的英语专业本科教育以及其间前往多伦多大学的交换经历让我对文学研究产生了浓厚的兴趣。而这样的兴趣能够在本科毕业之时得到即时的延续与大师的指导，是我莫大的荣幸和幸福。

　　我对于"文学经典与个人创新"这一主题的研究兴趣萌发于著名汉学家罗多弼教授2011年秋季在香港城市大学做访问学者时所教授的课程《文学中的语言》。课程的文本之一便是T. S.艾略特的《什么是经典？》。其中有关文学经典与个人创新两者关系的探讨引发了我最初浅显的思考：在创作过程中，创作者应该遵循传统还是注重出新？我的导师张隆溪教授在与我的日常交流与讨论中给予了我充分的鼓励和支持，引导我去寻找中西方文学评论中相关的理论探讨。四年的直博学习中，张老师给予我重要的方向引领的同时，尊重我自己的想法，注重培养我自主研究的意识与能力。在这精准有力的指导背后，是他广泛的阅读范围与渊博的知识储备，以及对中西比较文学研究的深入了解与准确把握。他的支持与肯定，让我坚信"文学经典与个人创新"这一主题是可挖掘、可研究的，有丰富的前期研究资源与研究基础，又有潜在的、衍生的新问题与新挑战。有关于这一主题的后

V

续研究，也证明了这一点。

"经典"不仅仅是中西文学批评中都有所触及的理论概念，也不只是具体的经典作品，更是21世纪世界文学背景下的一种研究意识，或是研究模式。在张老师的建议下，我寻找了中西方文学批评中有关经典与创新的相关讨论，从西方文评中的柏拉图，蒲柏，尼采，王尔德，T. S. 艾略特与温伯格，到中国文学批评中的陆机，刘勰，严羽，袁枚和钱钟书，文学批评者对于这一问题的理论讨论突破了时空的界限，默契地采用了辩证的角度论证了一个相似的结论：盲从经典会限制创新，学习经典却可以指导创新。本书的第一、第二章便是纵向与横向维度的理论梳理，呈现经典与创新辩证关系的相关观点在中西方文学批评中的起源，互动与发展脉络。

经典与创新相辅相成这一理论性结论为应对现代以来经典作为具体的文学作品体系在现实研究实践中所遇到的问题与挑战提供了理论指导。本书的第三章列举了这些问题与挑战：伍尔夫笔下受到女性创作挑战的男性主导的经典作品；哈罗德·布鲁姆笔下排斥文化研究等新兴学科染指的文学经典作品；以及在世界文学兴起的今天，被质疑的、局限于西方语言与文化的文学经典作品等。在承接了前两章所得出的理论总结基础上，此章旨在倡导更包容、更开放的文学经典作品体系。

经典不仅仅是具体的概念或作品，更是一种研究模式与研究意识。在多样性和流动性被充分推崇的今天，经典的理论定义不再是唯一的，经典作品体系也不再一成不变。当我们谈及经典，我们不能再理所当然地展开讨论，而应在解决一系列基本问题的基础上进行：首先，什么是经典？如何甄别与判断新创作的文学作品是否经典，以及如何看待外来文化及语言的文学经典作品？其次，如何阐释经典？如何合理利用本文化与本民族的角度去重新阐释外来的文学经典或新兴的文学经典，如何避免错误地、狭隘地或带有偏见地阐释外来文学经典？最后，如何阅读与传播经典？如何选择经典的阅读方式，固守文本细读还是大规模、数据化的分析？如何在翻译等新文学经典传播方式中完整而辩证地保留或利用文学经典？

本书的第四、五章以具体的文本研究案例与现时的理论讨论为基础，集中探讨了如何阐释经典以及如何传播与阅读经典这两个问题。第四章以莎士比亚的经典作品《暴风雨》以及塞泽尔的法语改编作品《一个暴风雨》为例，探讨如何在复杂多变的研究背景下，鼓励正确而多样的阐释角度。这一题目受启发于柯夏智教授在香港城市大学所开设的课程《跨文化研究》。柯夏智教授在课程中介绍了《暴风雨》的后殖民解读，列举了其中针对卡利班为代表的殖民地原住民负面描述的文本证据，并说明了后殖民解读带给《暴风雨》的严重后果——被禁止进入教学课堂，进而引出了塞泽尔所创作的、反殖民歧视、将卡利班英雄化的改编作品《一个暴风雨》。而我出于对文学经典被拒于课室之外的遗憾，着手从《暴风雨》后殖民解读的起源与发展历史出发，质疑其作为唯一阐释角度的合理性，以中西文学理论中有关经典多样性、包容性的论述为基础，倡导多角度共存的经典阐释方法。

而第五章则选择了脚注这一特殊、有趣的研究对象，呈现其在世界文学繁荣发展的新背景下作为一种新工具、新方法在文学经典阅读、研究与传播的过程中所扮演的重要角色。世界文学无疑是当今文学研究的重要命题。文化交流日益繁盛的今天，我们关注到了更多文化背景下的文学作品，就像世界文学概念提出者歌德有机会阅读来自大陆另一边的中国小说一样。然而，面对来自不同文化背景、多语言创作、数量浩繁的文学作品，我们是否有精力、能力及时间全部细读、研究并精通呢？弗兰克·莫莱蒂在其著名理论文章《世界文学猜想》中提出以"泛读"作为阅读与研究世界文学的方法，引发了学界的热烈讨论。而我却被文章中篇幅冗长到异乎寻常的脚注所吸引。莫莱蒂提出以一个具体的主题或问题为引领，统筹相关的国别文学作品与已有研究结论作为佐证来阐释相关主题与问题的结论，而脚注便成为呈现这些作品和佐证的新方式。同样，脚注在文学经典作品的翻译与传播中也大有作为。大卫·丹莫若什指出，在翻译和传播文学经典作品的过程中，有些必要的文化背景知识需要提供给非本文化背景的读者。而脚注便成为提供这些信息的重要工具。翻译中冗长而复杂的脚注并没有被读者惧怕或排斥,反而变得越来越被人接受,并且成为重要的阅读与理解的辅助手段。

事实上,本书的立意,以及每一章的内容,都与21世纪世界文学的研究背景息息相关,这也是我要在题目中加入"世界文学背景下"这一限定短语的原因。世界文学无疑是当今文学研究的重要命题。今天的我们所面对的文学经典作品与文学研究已经不再仅仅来自某一语言,某一国别甚至某一文化背景,而是多语言,多国别与多元文化背景的。而这些多样、多元的文学经典作品与研究,也并不仅仅是独立于彼此以个体的形式存在,而是相互关联、相互交流、相互融合,形成了跨语言、跨国别与跨文化背景的新整体与新形态。在这样的新形态中,正如我之前提到的,我们总会面临新的命题与新的挑战。因此,虽然关于经典的兴趣起源于理论探讨,但是我更愿意以世界文学背景下所产生的新问题为出发点,以探寻与论证解决问题的方法与角度为目的,追溯先前的理论讨论与现实问题,寻求理论指导与实践经验。在理论梳理中,我选择了中西文学批评理论中关于经典的讨论,在对比中看到这两个看似疏远的理论体系产出了高度契合的理论结论;在回顾现实问题的过程中,我选取了性别对立、学科壁垒与文化差异等挑战在经典研究中的实践案例,为之后探讨21世纪世界文学背景下如何解决文学经典研究中的新问题、新挑战提供了实践参考。当然,本书中理论探讨与现实问题的选择未必面面俱到,希望所得出的结论能够给关注文学经典这一命题的研究者们一些参考与帮助。近年来,我很高兴地看到文学经典及其理论与实践意义这一话题得到了很多国内学者的关注,希望今后能有更多的交流,让这一研究问题得到补充与延展。

感谢我的导师张隆溪教授一如既往的支持与鼓励,他慷慨地分享他的所学,并以严于律己的学术精神与温润如玉的大师脾性影响着我,这些于我都是最大的裨益。同时,也要感谢我的本科论文指导老师王宁教授,他的鼓励让我对外国文学的热爱与思考得以萌芽、成长;感谢我的师兄张万民教授在香港期间对我学习和生活的帮助;感谢我的同事广东外语外贸大学(以下简称"广外")的刘岩教授推荐"博学文库"项目并鼓励我积极申请。很荣幸能够入选这一项目。说起来,我与外教社的缘分也不止于此。2015年9月,在我刚刚从香港城市大学毕业来到广外任教时,我便代表广外参加了由外教社主办的第六届"外教社"杯全国高校外语教学比赛,并获得了广东赛区的一等奖。如今,有幸在外教社出版我的第一部学术著作,教研相长,与有荣焉,感谢外教社给予我的机会与肯定。也感谢广外多年来的培养与支持。同时,感谢广外外国文学文化研究院《中西比较视野下文学经典意义的再思考:诗学讨论与实践研究》项目的支持。

最后,感谢我的家人,他们的陪伴与支持是我前进道路上不可或缺的力量。

蒋竹雨

广东外语外贸大学英语语言文化学院副教授、硕士生导师
广东外语外贸大学阐释学研究院兼职研究员
2022年12月24日

Contents

Introduction

It seems that when the word *classic* is mentioned, it should always be accompanied by the definite article, *the*. *The classic* is considered the accurate and common way to use the word. And normally, when we encounter this term, we naturally expect it to mean a fixed list of literary works. Such an expectation is certainly understandable and valid. The first entry for *classic* in the *Oxford English Dictionary*, for example, defines it as "An ancient Greek or Latin writer or literary work."[1] But what I want convey here by using the word *classic* is not any fixed list or any specific set of literary works but rather a sense of the past in literary creation and literary studies. It can be interpreted as a gesture to refer to and preserve the past and precedent literary works in our new literature creation. Synonyms such as *canon* and *tradition* can also work in this sense but not as well as *classic*. *Canon*, with its original meaning as "a measuring rod" (qtd. in Carravetta 264), seems to indicate a list that is fixed and inflexible. It is more a fixed list of literary works that excludes or even discriminates against other classic works and new works. *The classic,* conversely, can be taken as a more tolerant and open concept. Unlike *canon*, which can be limited and biased, *tradition* may be too broad a concept for my discussion here. *Tradition* can refer not only to that of literature or that of academic studies; it is more of a cultural term than a literary term. Compared to these two terms, *the classic* is more appropriate for my discussion.

Contrary to the sense of past that *the classic* conveys, *creativity* represents the strength of the new and the original in literary creation. It implies a detachment and break from the past and the precedent. It emphasizes individual and

---

[1] "classic, adj. and n." *OED Online*. Oxford University Press, December 2014. Web. 30 January 2015.

personal aspects, and it is often taken as a contrast to the collective personality or common tastes that have been reflected through literary classic works. And unlike literary classics, which can be familiarized through cultivation and education, creativity cannot be deliberately acquired. It can be subjective emotions or feelings that are spontaneous; it can be the genius and talent with which some fortunate individuals are gifted or endowed; and it can be the divine inspiration that cannot be obtained through human effort. Creativity therefore acts as a counterpart to the classic in literary creation.

The classic and creativity have always had a paradoxical relationship with each other. On one hand, the classic nurtures creativity. Great minds and their profound thoughts preserved in the great masterpieces have enlightened generations of readers and writers. Figures of prominence are readily presented to us. Their insight and intelligence nurture our minds and tastes, and their achievements enable us to make further progress. The classic directs and inspires individual creativity. On the other hand, as some have argued, the classic may also impede creativity. The cultivation of the classics seems to be a forced requisite for those who strive for innovation and originality. The influence of the classics can be so irresistible and their popularity is so overwhelming that every single work that is labeled as individual or creative may be overshadowed. To some, the classic can be shackles to the development of individual creativity. It may even threaten the survival of creative works. It proves hard for literary works that are claimed as new to garner approval among an audience that is already familiar with the classic. Therefore, it becomes even harder to read the classic with a stream of skepticism and to bring change and reform to the existing canon of the classic.

Such a paradoxical relationship between the classic and creativity has been revealed and supported by discussions from cultures and literatures across geographical and linguistic borders. If we examine ideas about the classic and creativity in Chinese and Western literary criticism, we can find unexpected affinities. When tracing the origin of literature or poetry, Plato (429? BCE–347 BCE) attributes poetic creation to supernatural and divine power. He argues that the creation of poetry is dominated by inspiration instead of reason. He depicts a poet as "a light and winged thing, and holy, and never able to compose until he has become inspired, and is beside himself and reason is no longer in him" (Plato, *The Dialogues of Plato* 220). Similarly, in Chinese literary criticism, Liu Xie (or Liu Hsieh, 465?–520?) suggests that "*wen*, or pattern, is a very great power indeed" and that "it is born with Heaven and Earth" (Liu 8). When illuminating the purpose of poetry, the "Mao" preface to *The Book of Poetry* suggests that "the Ode is where the aim [*zhi*] goes" and that "while in the heart [*xin*], it is the aim; manifested in words, it is an Ode" (Zoeren 95). Poetry therefore features creativity and subjectivity. Resonating voices can also be heard in Western literary criticism. William Wordsworth (1770–1850), for example, suggests that "all good poetry is the spontaneous overflow of powerful feelings," which can be traced back to the inherent personality of poets (Wordsworth et al. 8). The significance of the classic is also acknowledged by both Chinese and Western literary critics. When Yan Yu (1192/1197?–1241/1245?) explains why the cultivation of the classic and tradition is essential for poets to initiate their production of masterpieces, he suggests that "judgment is the dominant factor in the study of poetry" and that "the beginning must be correct, and your mind must be set on the highest goals" (qtd. in Owen, *Readings in Chinese Literary Thought* 394). Correspondingly, when T. S. Eliot (1888–1965) suggests that "no poet, no artist of any art, has his complete meaning alone. His significance, his appreciation is the appreciation of his relation to the dead poets and artists," he must be referring to the everlasting, overwhelming, and indispensable influence of tradition and the classic in literary creation (*The Sacred Wood* 49). Affinities in ideas have also appeared in discussions between contemporary writers and critics. When addressing his audience at a banquet as a Nobel laureate, Ernest Hemingway (1899–1961) declared that "a true writer ... should always try for something that has never been done or that others have tried and failed" (Hemingway). He also attributed his achievement to his predecessors' efforts, as he said that "it is because we have had such great writers in the past that a writer is driven far out past where he can go, out to where no one can help him" (Ibid.). Like Hemingway, Mo Yan (1955–), another Nobel laureate, notices how both the classic and creativity function in the process of creating literature. To emphasize the consistency in inheriting the classic mind, he describes in his banquet speech a kind of "hearts beating in unison" (Mo). He suggests that "one writer influences another when they enjoy a profound spiritual kinship" (Ibid.). At the same time, he also insists that "the process of creation is unique to every writer" and that "each of my novels differs from the others in terms of plot and guiding inspiration" (Ibid.).

Although the relationship between the classic and creativity is paradoxical, the Chinese and Western ideas have been consistent in expounding it. In fact, to compare and correlate discussions from Chinese and Western literary criticism is not only to answer and elaborate on an important question in literary studies with more evidence and references but also to make different cultures connect and communicate with each other, which is more illuminating and constructive in this age of world literature. To discuss the question of the classic and creativity by referring to Chinese and Western literary criticism is to break the barriers established because of the provincial prejudice against the "other" cultures. Such a comparison and correlation serve as a rebuttal against attempts or claims that dichotomize and even downgrade cultures and literatures. From the discussion, we will find that affinities in thinking and mutual understanding are applicable not only within the same community, in which people share a similar cultural cultivation, but also when it comes to the question of bridging different cultures and literatures. Differences between cultures cannot be disregarded, but they are not reasons to deconstruct and defeat affinities that exist between different cultures. Exaggerating and emphasizing differences to an unreasonable level and making cultures into dichotomies should be avoided in this age of world literature.

Zhang Longxi rebuts F. L. Lucas's claim that only Greeks who have inherited the expected "curiosity and capability" are qualified to enquire into and articulate questions such as what is the origin of literature ("Poetics and World Literature" 327). Such a statement unreasonably emphasizes cultural uniqueness and superiority, differentiating cultures and disregarding their correlation. Zhang's refutation of this is supported by his erudite and solid references from different cultures and languages, the elaborations of which enlighten us about the fundamental questions of the poetics of literature.

One of the key questions concerning the origin of literature is the paradoxical interaction between the classic and creativity. To address these issues, Zhang Longxi suggests that we should acknowledge "the diversity as well as the affinities across different traditions" but not indulge ourselves in the rigid adherence to a national and regional literary tradition (Ibid.). This will generate new insights and facilitate better and deeper explorations of these questions.

In the process of comparing different cultures, however, some deliberately disregard the cultural affinities and confine themselves to the discovered differences. This results in unreasonable and even monstrous prejudice against certain cultures. Dichotomies and extreme differences between different cultures are what such critics achieve and advocate. Chinese culture and literature, for example, are always readily assumed to be the opposite of culture and literature in the Western world. The geographical distance between China and the Western world seems to be the perfect excuse to argue for the definite incompatibility of the two cultures. Michel Foucault (1926–1984), for example, once fictionalized Chinese culture as "the ultimate other":

> There would appear to be, then, at the other extremity of the earth we inhabit, a culture entirely devoted to the ordering of space, but one that does not distribute the multiplicity of existing things into any of the categories that make it possible for us to name, speak, and think. (qtd. in Zhang Longxi, *Mighty Opposites* 20)

The fictionalized China as heterotopia developed by Foucault here, as Zhang argues, enables him "to differentiate the self from what is alien and pertaining to the Other and to map out the contours of Western culture recognizable as a self-contained system" (Zhang Longxi, *Mighty Opposites* 21). To deconstruct the illusory prejudice against a distant culture and to construct the accessible and achievable tunnel in between are urgent and necessary in this age of world literature. What I want to emphasize here is the need to find the unexpected affinities between two seemingly distant cultures by comparing and discussing questions that intrigue the whole of human kind, not just a closed community. Questions about the classic and creativity deserve comparative and global

6 perspectives and approaches. Ideas from both China and the West contribute to the answers to this poetical and philosophical question. We can certainly find differences: Even when we examine the question along the historical continuum within the same culture, opinions and ideas can diverge subject to different times, contexts, and individual experiences and personalities. Affinities, however, cannot be disregarded. Even between two different cultures, we can find consistency in ideas and discussions. Corresponding ideas can even be illuminated by each other, regardless of the assumed distance and unfamiliarity between these two cultures.

Although the paradoxical relationship between the classic and creativity has been adequately analyzed and supported by arguments made by literary critics from different cultures, some still deliberately ignore it or only partially recognize and emphasize one aspect of it. The classic, for example, is sometimes reduced to a biased "means of discrimination" that suppresses and eliminates creativity. When T. S. Eliot tried to emphasize the importance of cultivating a sense of the past, he suggested that poets go through a process of depersonalization, within which there is a "continual surrender," a "continual self-sacrifice," and "a continual extinction of personality" (*The Sacred Wood* 30). Eliot also suggested that the concept of "maturity," which enables the production of masterpieces, cannot be apprehended by an "immature" individual mind ("What Is a Classic" 10). The classic is not only mistaken as a measure to exclude individual talent in general, but it is also sometimes wrongly taken as a means of discriminating against female creativity. Virginia Woolf (1882–1941), in her book *A Room of One's Own,* describes how the classic works "celebrate male virtues, enforce male values and describe the world of men," and she sarcastically suggests that "the emotion with which these books are permeated is to a woman incomprehensible" (Woolf 77). The classic can also perform discriminating and eliminating acts to new disciplines. The classic, to some scholars, should remain a closed and elite concept that is not to be violated by emerging disciplines. Harold Bloom (1930–2019), for example, in his book *The Western Canon,* defends the gesture of keeping the classic and canon in the closed realm of aesthetic studies, and he loathes the intrusion of "cultural criticism" into the study of the classic (Bloom 17). The worst of all the acts of discrimination in which the classic engages is against cultures. Both Pascale Casanova and Franco Moretti, for example, argue that there is an "unequal" literary system in the world, within which there is a "core" culture and the "periphery" cultures (Moretti 56) and "literary domination" (Casanova xii). The classic from the assumed "core" culture is therefore superior and exclusive compared to the classic from other cultures and literatures.

The classic should not be exclusive or discriminating; rather, it should be inclusive and tolerant. The classic should be open to the creativity of different individuals and genders and should not reject perspectives and interpretations that are new and different. It should embrace contributions from diverse disciplinary and cultural backgrounds. The problem, however, concerns the following questions. Should the classic be tolerant enough to accept any contribution made by creativity? Are all newly created works convincing and reasonable? Should the classic be transformed whenever new perspectives are introduced? Should the classic lose its origin through the metamorphosis? Should creativity be regarded as the supreme, and should the classic be completely subject to creativity?

Such problems become more obvious in this age of world literature. The communication and circulation of the classic works that are developed within different cultural and historical backgrounds prosper on a level that has never been achieved before. Readers have access to foreign literatures, and their curiosity and desire for an exotic taste can be satisfied. The problem, however, is that people born and bred within different cultures must have different perspectives for approaching the same piece of classic literature. Audiences from the original culture cannot anticipate the interpretation of the classic adopted by the target audience in a different culture. It is highly likely that people will change and transform the classic so as to make it fit in with the target context and cater to a certain political regime. During this process, a piece of a classic work is to be detached from its origins. Sometimes such assimilation can be so irrational that the classic loses its original and fundamental meanings and values.

Adaptation is a popular way to assimilate and transform a classic work. Aimer Cesaire (1913–2008), for example, creatively and critically adapted

Shakespeare's classic play *The Tempest* into his new play *A Tempest*, resonating with the claim that "Shakespeare meant *The Tempest* to be substantially about English imperialism, to take place in English America (perhaps even in Bermuda)" (Vaughan and Vaughan 5). Cesaire accuses *The Tempest* of intending to boost colonialism. Yet some scholars applaud the postcolonial indications of *The Tempest*. Peter Hulme, for example, insists that "The postcolonial readings of *The Tempest* are not better just because they tend to be more interesting" but "they both read the play better, and read the misreadings of others" (Hulme). To Hulme, postcolonial reading can confer the exclusive title to study *The Tempest,* and with proficiency in this specialized field, scholars can certainly exhaust the study of the play. Since this monstrous transformation, *The Tempest* has become a classic play for postcolonial reading only, which is a pathetic fact and a great loss for Shakespearean readers and scholars. This kind of creativity ghettoizes cultures and literatures, which is unfeasible and unacceptable in the age of world literature.

Footnoting is also a way for creativity to wrestle with the classic. Footnotes that contain references to the classic and tradition reflect T. S. Eliot's obsession with the classic; however, footnotes can also constitute subjective interpretation and comments that transform the classic. Footnotes to, or rather commentaries on, *The Book of Poetry*, for example, contain personal and subjective understandings and remarks that assimilate the classic poetry collection into different political regimes.

The struggle between the classic and creativity in footnotes has become more complicated in this age of world literature. Franco Moretti, for instance, initiates a "wave" project in which we create a "general pattern" in the "production and reception" of world literature to summarize different literatures (qtd. in Pizer 3). Classics from different cultures are therefore situated within the subjectively created scheme of world literature. To make the project successful, Moretti suggests a method of "distant reading," which means reading "a patchwork of other people's research, without a single direct textual reading" (Moretti 57). References to "periphery" cultures are therefore situated in the marginal footnotes. Such a gesture, of course, prompts controversy and criticism. Footnotes in translations also indicate the struggle between the classic and creativity. Whether we should be faithful to the classic and preserve the original piece in translations as much as possible or whether we should create translations that completely assimilate the classic so as to please the target readers is an issue that needs to be addressed. David Damrosch's discussion on the translation of *The Tale of Genji*, for example, reflects how translators struggle with such a dilemma ("World Literature, National Contexts" 521–522).

Chapter One

The Classic and Creativity in Western Literary Criticism

1.1   Poetry and Inspiration: The Paradoxical Plato ——

The concept of the classic can be inclusive. Sometimes it is used to represent human intelligence, and sometimes it corresponds to tradition, but both human intelligence and tradition emphasize the consistency and constancy of a certain literary custom that was established by the human mind and human effort. Meanwhile, it is sometimes compared with nature, which embodies the supreme authority. The ideas about individual talent and creativity can also be complicated and divided. They may refer to the subjective feeling, reasoning, and thinking of individuals. They can also mean inspiration, gift, and genius, which, when contrasted with the former aspects, are unconscious and supernatural. They are beyond the reach and control of human beings. How these elements interact and relate to each other is an important question to be addressed in order to illustrate the relationship between the classic and creativity.

Returning to the acknowledged origin of Western literature and culture, we find that inquiry into the origin of poetry or literature has already been initiated. In the world of ancient Greece, when philosophical awareness and thinking emerged and developed, the paradoxical relationship between the classic and creativity did not escape philosophers' attention. What they considered counterparts in literary creation, however, are not the same as what we consider them to be today. The two elements compared are not the classic and creativity. Their discussion is developed and extended from their assumptions about the interaction between poetry and inspiration. Compared to creativity, which was derived from human beings themselves, inspiration in ancient Greece seemed to be detached from human beings but was subject to something that is supernatural and mysterious. It was beyond human beings' control and understanding. To some ancient Greek philosophers, poetry was therefore not formulated by or for human subjectivity but was created under divine inspiration. It was unlike what we normally understand as the classic today, which are always attributed to individual talent or originality.

Plato (429? BCE–347 BCE), as one of the acknowledged masters and beginners of Western culture and literature, should not be ignored. Plato's attitudes toward poetry and inspiration are confusing and complicated. He does not take sides with either poetry or inspiration; rather, he seems unable to be consistent and clear about his side. He admits that inspiration sheds light on poetry and endows the poet with a great gift; however, he also condemns inspiration because it deprives poets of their rationality and wisdom. Through his discussion and assertion, we can see the paradoxical relationship between poetry and inspiration. Plato touches upon the relationship between poetry and inspiration in several of his works. On one hand, Plato holds negative attitudes toward poetry and inspiration. In *Apology*, he claims that poets can only create poetry when they are deprived of rationality and inspired by instinct, suggesting that "it was not wisdom that enabled them to write their poetry, but a kind of instinct or inspiration, such as you find in seers and prophets" (Plato, *The Dialogues of Plato* 8). This implies that poetry is not "composed through wisdom, which explains the incapability of poets to elaborate their own poems and which renders the status of poets degrading and humiliating" (Murray 10). On the other hand, he seems to acknowledge the sacredness of inspiration. He describes the poet as "a light and winged thing, and holy, and never able to compose until he has become inspired, and is beside himself and reason is no longer in him" (Plato, *Plato's Phaedrus* 60). He confesses that "the greatest blessings come by way of madness, indeed of madness that is Heaven-sent" (Ibid. 56). In fact, Plato holds such paradoxical attitudes toward poetry and inspiration because of his disagreement with the common view before and at his time. To some scholars, the divine origin is *12* a positive indicator of poetry, as "it is used to guarantee its truth and quality" (Murray 10). As Murray suggests in his book *Plato on Poetry*:

> From Homer onwards poets invoke the Muses' aid, calling on them, as daughters of Memory, to provide them with knowledge, to instill sweetness into their song, or to assist them generally in the composition and performance of their poems. Poetry is regularly portrayed as a divine gift, which the Muses bestow or teach. (Ibid. 7)

It seems that inspiration is a divine gift that is to be bestowed and worshipped. Poets who are lucky enough to be gifted cannot achieve the same through deliberate attempts to grab inspiration by themselves. Inspiration is a positive and crucial element for the creation of poetry.

Another reason for inspiration being held as indispensable for poetry is that it is consistent with the concept of craft and wisdom. As Murray suggests, "hand in hand with the notion of inspiration goes the idea of poetry as a craft" (Ibid. 8). Poetry, under this circumstance, becomes more related to poetics, the concept of which is more familiar to us today. *Poetics* refers to the more technical, more manageable parts of poems, such as meter, diction, melody, and rhythm. Aristotle (384 BCE–322 BCE), for example, suggests that poetry is produced because of the human instinct of mimesis (*Poetics* 37). It "distinguishes them from other animals: man is the most mimetic of all, and it is through mimesis that he develops his earliest understanding" (Ibid.). Therefore, how to make the mimesis vivid and superior depends on the techniques and strategies of poets. Poets can use metaphors, similes, and other possible figures of speech. They can also elaborately design the meter and rhythm of their poems. How to assemble them and how to apply them beautifully and appropriately requires poets' familiarity with the elements and experience in using them. This is why poets are respected as craftsmen:

> By the end of the fifth century we find the poet himself referred to as a *poietes* (maker), and his art as a *techne*. Thus in pre-Platonic literature poets are portrayed both as *sophoi*, "wise men," who have access to knowledge through the inspiration of the Muses, and as skilled craftsmen. (Murray 8)

Plato, however, seems inclined to emphasize the passivity and negativity of poetry caused by inspiration. His intention is to "provide an overwhelming image of irrationality, at least so far as the poetic process is concerned" (Ibid. 9). The irrationality of the poetry is the determinant that results in the paradoxical feature of inspiration. On one hand, the better the poems, the more irrational they are. Irrationality is the symbol of divine inspiration bestowed on poets. On the other hand, irrationality deprives poets of their techniques. They have little knowledge of the mechanics of the composition in their work, nor can they reasonably explain and analyze their poems. As Murray summarizes,

> Plato transforms the traditional notion of poetic inspiration by emphasizing the passivity of the poet and the irrational nature of the poetic process. He differs most significantly from his predecessors in maintaining that inspiration is incompatible with *techne*. (Ibid.)

It is the lack of rationality of poets that Plato consistently attacks. Inspiration may be a divine gift that enables poets to achieve what they cannot access with their own reasoning and thinking, but it can also deprive poets of their knowledge and wisdom. Plato's paradoxical attitude toward the creation of poetry is thus formed. A. N. Whitehead once commented that "the safest general characterization of the European philosophical tradition is that it consists of a series of footnotes to Plato" (39). Similarly, if we continue to explore how the classic and creativity interact with each other in the process of literary creation, we can easily find that most scholars adopt paradoxical attitudes toward the classic and creativity, which are derived from Plato's idea and are consistent with him.

1.2 Pope: "Nature and Homer Were the Same"

Alexander Pope (1688–1744), for example, delivers similar ideas in his long and intricate poem "An Essay on Criticism." Pope notices the antithesis between inspiration and cultivation. He admits that something beyond human

14 capability impacts literary creation and appreciation, but he reminds us that tradition and the classic also influence individual production of literature and personal tastes of literary criticism. Instead of making them dichotomies, however, Pope prefers a synthesis of the two aspects. Another difference is that, unlike Plato, who focuses on the negative effect of inspiration and emphasizes the negative aspects of the paradoxical relationship between inspiration and poetry, Pope promotes a harmonious combination of the two. Pope does not attribute inspiration to any supernatural powers or mythical existences; rather, he considers "nature" the equal of inspiration and takes tradition and the classic, for example, "Homer," as its counterpart. The supreme authority and assistance that nature bestows on writers and critics can be as important as the constructive guidance and influence received from literary classics. Both are indispensable, and both are helpful. Pope encourages people to pay attention to the positive interaction and communication between the two rather than focus on the conflict and compromise between the two. Here is an excerpt about nature, taken from Pope's "An Essay on Criticism":

> First follow NATURE, and your Judgment frame
> By her just Standard, which is still the same:
> Unerring Nature, still divinely bright,
> One clear, unchang'd and Universal Light,
> Life, Force, and Beauty, must to all impart,
> At once the Source, and End, and Test of Art
> Art from that Fund each just Supply provides,
> Works without Show, and without Pomp presides:
> In some fair Body thus th' informing Soul
> With Spirits feeds, with Vigour fills the whole,
> Each Motion guides, and ev'ry Nerve sustains; (Pope 38)

Pope suggests that nature has the capability to impart "life, force and beauty" to art. Literary creation and appreciation is refined and regulated by nature. Nature constitutes and functions as "the source, and end, and text of art" (Ibid.). Pope points out that nature abides by its own law, to which other existences in the world also conform (Ibid.). From the above quotation, we can also see that nature, in Pope's opinion, is a divine symbol, functioning no less miraculously than the Muse in literary creation and criticism. To acquire a better judgment and refined taste of literature depends on nature, which is "just," "unerring," "divinely bright," "clear," and "universal" (Ibid.). Nature is like the unconscious inspiration in Plato's discussion about poetry. Both are beyond the scope of human thinking and reasoning.

Plato suggests that because of inspiration, poets are deprived of rationality and therefore cannot reasonably apply "*techne*" and "craft" to their poetry. Pope also notices the importance of "*techne*." When appreciating and explaining a poem, poets are required to make clear and just comments. To accomplish this, as Pope proceeds with his argument in his long poem, poets need to refer to the classic and tradition:

> You then whose Judgment the right Course wou'd steer,
> Know well each ANCIENT's proper Character,
> His Fable, Subject, Scope in ev'ry Page,
> Religion, Country, Genius of his Age:
> Without all these at once before your Eyes,
> Cavil you may, but never Criticize.
> Be Homer's Works your Study, and Delight,
> Read them by Day, and meditate by Night,
> Thence form your Judgment, thence your Maxims bring,
> And trace the Muses upward to their Spring;
> Still with It self compar'd, his Text peruse;
> And let your Comment be the Mantuan Muse. (Ibid. 39)

> When first young Maro in his boundless Mind
> A Work t' outlast Immortal Rome design'd,
> Perhaps he seem'd above the Critick's Law,
> And but from Nature's Fountains scorn'd to draw:
> But when t'examine ev'ry Part he came,
> Nature and Homer were, he found, the same:
> Convinc'd, amaz'd, he checks the bold Design,

And Rules as strict his labour'd Work confine,

As if the Stagyrite o'er looked each Line.

16
Learn hence for Ancient Rules a just Esteem;

To copy Nature is to copy Them. (Ibid. 39–40)

To learn from "Homer" and "Ancient's proper character" benefits writers and critics. This "right course" "steers" our judgment and tastes. We should "know well" the tradition and the classic. To receive education from the classic and tradition is a pleasure, as Homer is not only our "study" but also a "delight." We "read" the classic; we "mediate" to gain more from the classic.

Pope neither denies the importance of the classic nor downgrades the divine and inspirational value of nature. He suggests the simultaneity and the similarity of both, as he concludes that "Nature and Homer were, he found, the same" and that "to copy Nature is to copy Them" (Ibid. 40). Pope's inclination to establish a harmonious and reciprocal relationship between "Nature" and "Homer" is not simply a pluralistic resolution; it is rather an alternative perspective for approaching the paradoxical relationship between these counterparts in literary creation. Plato focuses more on the struggle between inspiration and poetry, while Pope emphasizes the affinities between nature and Homer. Michael Bruce therefore suggests,

> Pope is the liberal neoclassicist who respects Horace's recommended "decorum," but never at the expense of that inspired moment of poetic passion which "gloriously offend[s]" to "snatch a grace beyond the reach of art." Pope's commitment to tradition encouraged him to normalize the idiosyncratic; he had no intention, however, of circumscribing genius by "dull receipts." (Bruce 268)

1.3 Wordsworth: Thoughts Are the Representatives of Past Feelings

Pope's idea reminds us of William Wordsworth's (1770–1850) opinion. As the iconic figure of the school of Romanticism, Wordsworth highly praises the importance of innate feelings and personal perceptions in the creation of poetry. The "spontaneous overflow of powerful feelings" is the most commonly acknowledged and representative phrase of Romanticism (Wordsworth et al. 8). It seems that Wordsworth is different from Plato and Pope, who attribute literary creation to supernatural and mythical powers such as Muse and almighty nature, because Wordsworth emphasizes human beings themselves; however, if we look carefully at Wordsworth's view of poetry creation, we can find similarities between him and Pope and Plato. Although the emphasis on individual feelings is related to human beings, it still reveals something that is detached from human reasoning and human will. Subjective feelings can be stimulated against human consciousness by external elements that are beyond human control and mastery. They are not rational or manageable but uncertain and instant. In this sense, Wordsworth's idea resembles those of Pope and Plato. At the same time, emotional subjectivity is not the only element that determines how poets create poetry. Like Pope, Wordsworth also touches on how the classic and tradition regulate and refine personal feelings that flourish in the individual creation of literature. This perspective adopted by Wordsworth is rarely noticed or discussed. The question is: how does Wordsworth address these two sides at the same time and include them both within the one key word, *feelings*?

The power bestowed by Wordsworth on the word *nature* is no less magnificent than the power of Pope's concept of nature. Nature, to Wordsworth, has a twofold meaning. First, nature is the material world, which serves as a sacred shrine of serenity for poets to pursue deeper mediation and to contemplate their primitive feelings and passions. Nature inspires poets not only in the sense that it stimulates their feelings and arouses their inner voices but also in the sense that it provides them with an ideal place to grasp the pure and original things and to perceive the innate emotions. Nature therefore serves as a sacred shrine for poets where they can mediate, just as Wordsworth argues in his renowned work "Preface to Lyrical Ballads": When situated within a natural world and a simple life, "the essential passions of the heart find a better soil in which they can attain their maturity, are less under restraint, and speak a plainer and more emphatic language" (Ibid.

7). Feelings germinated within this natural simplicity are "elementary" and harmonious; they will be "more accurately contemplated, and more forcibly communicated" (Ibid.). Passions are "more easily comprehended, and are more durable" (Ibid.). Within nature, poets will achieve a harmonious coexistence with nature, which is an elevated level for their creation, "because in that condition the passions of men are incorporated with the beautiful and permanent forms of nature" (Ibid.). To Wordsworth, nature also functions as an unerring criterion and standard to regulate and refine human beings' original feelings and emotions. As Wordsworth suggests, true poets strive to mirror genuine simplicity by choosing "incidents and situations from common life" (Ibid.). Poets describe the incidents with "language really used by men" (Ibid.), and, at the same time, poets "throw over them a certain coloring of imagination" (Ibid.). These gestures of poets, however, should never be detached from "the primary laws of our nature" (Ibid.).

Aside from representing the material world, nature can also indicate the inner and spiritual world of human minds. In fact, if we trace back to the definitions of *nature*, we can find an entry that corresponds to what Wordsworth means by *nature* here. In the *Oxford English Dictionary*, *nature* is defined as "senses relating to mental or physical impulses and requirements."[1] To further explore the definition to derive more details, we can find an item that reads "the inherent dominating power or impulse in a person by which character or action is determined, directed, or controlled."[2] *Nature* can refer to personal and subjective feelings that are generated within human beings. Men are conscious of such feelings, and they can deliberately apply such feelings to "character" or "action." How these feelings are stimulated and how they can be acquired, however, is beyond human grasp. They are more like inspiration in Plato's discussion and nature in Pope's argument. They are bestowed on human beings against human consciousness and cannot be cultivated intentionally. In fact,

---

[1] "Nature, n." *OED Online*. Oxford University Press, December 2014. Web. 31 January 2015.
[2] Ibid.

nature under this layer of meaning can be interpreted as either innate genius or as inner emotion. Yet, regardless of which aspect we emphasize, we will always notice that nature here is juxtaposed with cultivation and education, which are determined by acquired characteristics. Such a presumption can find support from another entry on *nature*, which defines it as "contrasted with nurture, esp. in nature and nurture: heredity and environment respectively as influences on, or determinants of, a person's personality or behavior."[1] The abstract and inherent power of "nature" is also contrasted with "action" and "behavior," which are the seeable and external performance that is manageable by human beings themselves. They are subjected to and determined by the "inherent," rather than the other way around. This reminds us of what Aristotle argues in *Poetics*. Aristotle holds a very different perspective. He suggests that the creation of poetry depends on human beings' craving to imitate. Aristotle uses the word *mimesis* to illustrate how poetry imitates an action or behavior. The reflection should be as accurate as the works of a "craftsman." The word is compared with *Phantasia,* created by Philostratus, meaning "a mental image" (Aristotle, *Poetics. Introduction, Commentary, and Appendixes* 258). This contradicts the definition of *nature* that we reviewed above. Nature as the inherent and innate is the dominant and steering power, and this definition can be referred to when we approach Wordsworth's discussion of poetry writing.

Romanticists, who favor inner voices, must not escape "nature" with such features. They prioritize "feelings" over "action" and "situation." Wordsworth emphasizes the significance of the "inherent" for poetry. He determines that "all good poetry is the spontaneous overflow of powerful feelings," which can be traced back to the inherent "organic sensibility" of poets (Wordsworth et al. 8). This is in stark contrast with "gross and violent stimulants," which belong to the external world (Ibid. 9). Not only does Wordsworth take the inherent as the essential ingredient and indispensable inspiration for poetry creation, but he also mentions how the inherent can have an impact on the external world. He suggests that "the feeling therein developed gives importance to the action

---

[1] "Nature, n." *OED Online*. Oxford University Press, December 2014. Web. 31 January 2015.

and situation, and not the action and situation to the feeling" (Ibid.). This can easily remind us of the definition given in the *Oxford English Dictionary*: "the inherent dominating power or impulse in a person by which character or action is determined, directed, or controlled." Feelings, emotions, passions, and sensibilities are all advantages that make poets superior to common people. As Wordsworth suggests, a poet is

> a man, it is true, endued with more lively sensibility, more enthusiasm and tenderness, who has a greater knowledge of human nature, and a more comprehensive soul, than are supposed to be common among mankind; a man pleased with his own passions and volitions, and who rejoices more than other men in the spirit of life that is in him. (Ibid. 13)

Although Wordsworth places supreme emphasis on innate feelings and internal voices, he does not create a dichotomy between "nature" and "nurture." The "spontaneous overflow of powerful feelings" does not indicate the wild expression of uncontrolled feelings. "Our continued influxes of feeling," as Wordsworth suggests, "are modified and directed by our thoughts, which are indeed the representatives of all our past feelings" (Ibid. 8). This resonates with Plato's idea about how inspiration deprives poets of their rationality. Strong feelings do not indicate irrationality, nor does the passion of poets entitle them to implement reckless and irresponsible catharsis. Rather, they are regulated and refined by our thoughts and reasoning. In addition, the passion of poets is not instant or overwhelming. Rather, it takes a milder, yet enduring form. Wordsworth suggests that "it takes its origin from emotion recollected in tranquility" (Ibid. 21) and that the recollections of emotion, through "repetition and continuance," gradually become "habits of mind" (Ibid. 8). He also suggests that "by obeying blindly and mechanically the impulses of these habits, we shall describe objects, and utter sentiments, of such a nature" (Ibid.). Such a process described by Wordsworth resembles that of cultivation. Reading and perceiving the literary classic is a tranquil moment when our feelings are first prompted. Constant and repetitive exposure to the classic makes us more sensitive to feelings that correspond between different classics, and our tastes and ability to find and appreciate the true excellence are gradually established and enhanced. Wordsworth suggests that "by contemplating the relation of these general representatives to each other, we discover what is really important to men, so, by the repetition and continuance of this act, our feelings will be connected with important subjects" (Ibid.). Our thoughts, which "are indeed the representatives of all our past feelings," are prompted, awakened, and refined by the classic (Ibid.). The classic works are representative of human minds that are selected by time and history. They are qualified to purify and improve our minds. What Wordsworth does here is to attach importance to the cultivation and nurturing of our feelings received from exposure to literary classics and traditions. He expressed "no dishonorable melancholy" about the negative tendency of his time. He suggests that men of his time produced "a craving for extraordinary incident" (Ibid. 9) and that this craving was unreasonably gratified. Even worse is that "to this tendency of life and manners the literature and theatrical exhibitions of the country have conformed themselves" (Ibid.). Wordsworth proceeds to utter his disagreement with and pity for this negative trend:

> The invaluable works of our elder writers, I had almost said the works of Shakespeare and Milton, are driven into neglect by frantic novels, sickly and stupid German Tragedies, and deluges of idle and extravagant stories in verse. When I think upon this degrading thirst after outrageous stimulation, I am almost ashamed to have spoken of the feeble endeavour made in these volumes to counteract it. (Ibid. 9–10)

To Wordsworth, the thirst for degrading stimulations makes people betray "the representative of all our past feelings." The craving for extraordinary incidents is detached from the excellence reflected through the classic, such as in the works of Shakespeare and Milton. Wordsworth therefore resonates with Pope and Plato in the sense that he notices the counterparts in the process of literary creation. Feelings and passions are indispensable for poets, but sensible thoughts and the conscious cultivation of the classic are also irreducible. They modify and direct our feelings.

1.4   Nietzsche: Apollonian and Dionysian

Romanticism inspired Friedrich Nietzsche (1844–1900). Raymond Geuss, in his introduction to the book *The Birth of Tragedy and Other Writings,* suggests that "the strand of response to this perceived problem that is most important for the genesis of Nietzsche's views is Romanticism" (Nietzsche, *Nietzsche* xiii). He supports such an assumption by quoting from Nietzsche himself: "As Nietzsche himself points out in the introduction to the second edition, *The Birth of Tragedy* is a work of Romanticism" (Ibid.). As Geuss proceeds with his introduction to the book, Nietzsche expresses nostalgia for "a highly idealized past" while, at the same time, "to highlight its contrast with and superiority to the 'modern' world" (Ibid.). Nietzsche seems to be more interested in reviving, reconstructing, and re-embodying the golden values of the past so as to be detached from the present.

Such a sense of the past seems to indicate his preference for the classic. "Archaic Greek society" is what Nietzsche is nostalgic about (Ibid.). To Nietzsche, it is "different from and superior to the modern world" (Ibid.). The reason why Nietzsche attaches importance to Greek culture is that Greek culture is "artistic." It is artistic not only in the sense that "it produced a lot of excellent art" but also in the sense that "it was in some sense fundamentally based on and oriented to art, not theoretical science or a formally codified morality" (Ibid.). It seems that Greek culture is more purified, aesthetic, humanistic, and emotional. To Nietzsche, Greek culture remains original and spontaneous, not having been refined or regulated by scientific thinking or moral teaching. It is emotional, personal, and original.

We always suppose that to be educated by the classic from the past makes people more cultivated. People will become more able to regulate their personal feelings, and they will acquire more rationality and reasoning to make better judgments rather than expressing their ideas wildly. Nietzsche's nostalgia for the classic and tradition, however, is not aroused by his craving for routine or reasoning but rather by his desire for spontaneity and originality.

Such an oxymoron also appears in Nietzsche's argument about the relationship between Apollonian and Dionysian. In *The Birth of Tragedy*, Nietzsche uses Apollo and Dionysus to represent respectively the "distinct moral individuals" and the "formless flux" or "intoxication" (Nietzsche, *The Birth of Tragedy* xvi). The Apollonian way is more rational and reserved. It "embodies the drive toward distinction, discreteness and individuality, toward the drawing and respecting of boundaries and limits; he teaches an ethic of moderation and self-control" (Nietzsche, *Nietzsche* xi). The Dionysian way, conversely, is wilder and more primitive. It is destined to destroy and defy. Geuss summarizes that "the Dionysiac is the drive towards the transgression of limits, the dissolution of boundaries, the destruction of individuality, and excess" (Ibid.).

It seems that the Apollonian way embodies and emphasizes the significance of the classic in literature, just as Geuss asserts that "in literature the purest and most intense expression of the Apolline is Greek epic poetry (especially Homer)" (Ibid.). People of Apollonian thinking must accord their tastes and judgment to rules and habits inherited and acquired from the classic and tradition. They respect the rules, and obey them. The Dionysian way, conversely, corresponds to individual creativity, which means to be singular and refreshing, disobeying traditions or rules and undermining limits and restrictions.

At the same time, Apollonian still represents individual aspects of people. Geuss argues that "the Apolline artist glorifies individuality by presenting attractive images of individual persons, things, and events" (Ibid.). The rationality and the obedience are not blind and unconscious submission. Apollonian still focuses on individuals. Similarly, Dionysian may still indicate some regulations and rules. "The purest artistic expression of the Dionysiac," as Geuss suggests, "was quasiorgiastic forms of music, especially choral singing and dancing" (Ibid.). Forms of music such as sonata-allegro follow certain rules and styles. Even the musical form "canon" features regulated repetitiveness. Dancing also features patterns and styles. Otherwise, the job of the choreographer would no longer be guaranteed. Such a paradoxical relationship unexpectedly resonates with and relates to the relationship between the classic and creativity.

24 In fact, the interaction between the two, as Nietzsche indicates, is indeed paradoxical: They contrast and complement each other. Despite his preference for the Dionysian drive, Nietzsche confesses that "without the counterbalance of the Apollonian, the Dionysian results in the pessimism and passivity of Indian Buddhism, convinced of the ultimate futility of individual existence" (Nietzsche, *The Birth of Tragedy* xix). The classic directs and refines individual creativity in the same way as the rational Apollonian mediates and regulates the wild Dionysian. Intoxicated and uncontrolled in emotions, Dionysian can be too wild and primitive to be accepted. It may offend readers due to the lack of rationality. Assisted by the disciplined and uniformed Apollonian, the Dionysian will learn to express their feelings in a less offensive and more acceptable way. In this way, individual creativity is to be realized in forms that have been testified and polished in the classic and tradition over years and generations. Cultivated by the classic and tradition, individual creativity will become more refined and regulated in the ways in which it is expressed. The contribution of individual creativity will be more convincible and acceptable.

1.5   Oscar Wilde: Unity Is of the Individual

Like Wordsworth, Oscar Wilde (1854–1900), another critic who enjoys worldwide renown, places emphasis on creativity. Wilde defends the importance of creativity and individuality. He calls on people to rebel against the authority of the classic and tradition. Rather than conform to the old, Wilde suggests, later generations should embrace and value creativeness. Although it is critics' rather than writers' creativity that Wilde argues about in "The Critic as Artist," Wilde's protective attitudes toward individual creativity and serious warning against the unexamined yet overwhelming impact of the classic and tradition can still be read between the lines. What Wilde promotes is critics' detachment from the past and authority. He praises the critics' creativity but loathes close attachment to and rigid confinement by the old and the past. Wilde devalues the fixed and irrefutable perspectives that have been established by the classic and tradition while at the same time validating the contribution of individual creativity, which should be freed from the submissive and yielding position beneath the authority of the classic and tradition.

Wilde prioritizes creativeness over the classic and tradition. Instead of analyzing how the classic and tradition influence individual creativity, Wilde reverses the causal relationship between the two by attributing the classic and tradition to the creativeness of individuals. As Gilbert suggests in "The Critic as Artist," an individual's poetic works only become poetry when "they have received a beautiful form ... For there is no art where there is no style, and no style where there is no unity, and unity is of the individual" (Wilde, *Collected Works of Oscar Wilde* 976). This "form" is by no means a shackle to confine creativeness, nor is it a set rule defined by the classic and tradition to impede individuality. The unity is not to be rigidly conformed to, either. It is never to cruelly generate individuality or impede creativity; rather, unity should be attributed to the creativeness of man. It is individual creativity that produces "the unity." Creativity is the base for unity. Just as Wilde's Gilbert in "The Critic as Artist" suggests,

> No doubt Homer had old ballads and stories to deal with, as Shakespeare had chronicles and plays and novels from which to work, but they were merely his rough material. He took them, and shaped them into song. They become his, because he made them lovely. (Ibid.)

Homer and Shakespeare are the classic figures with universal acknowledgment and prestige, but their works are only "the individual's" "rough material." It is only when the individual introduces his own view and creative perspective into the classic and tradition that they can be revitalized and lasting. Wilde summarizes,

> The longer one studies life and literature, the more strongly one feels that behind everything that is wonderful stands the individual, and that it is not the moment that makes the man, but the man who creates the age. Indeed, I am inclined to

think that each myth and legend that seems to us to spring out of the wonder, or terror, or fancy of tribe and nation, was in its origin the invention of one single mind. (Ibid. 979)

Individual creativeness seems to be the almighty element in literary creation and appreciation. In addition to emphasizing the superiority of the creativity of individuals, Wilde indicates that unreasonable faith in the classic and tradition blinds individual minds. He warns young people that being too attached to the old and the past will impede their intellectual maturity. In "The Critic as Artist," Gilbert suggests to Ernest,

> I am afraid that you have been listening to the conversation of someone older than yourself. That is always a dangerous thing to do, and if you allow it to degenerate into a habit, you will find it absolutely fatal to any intellectual development. (Ibid. 971)

Zhang Longxi, in his article "The Critical Legacy of Oscar Wilde," describes how Wilde disapproves of the precedent heritage when it comes to the development of individual creativity. He suggests that "for Wilde then, influence seems to be the power of an older and stronger personality that hinders and even cripples the development of personality of the younger, hence a power either to be shunned or countervailed" (Zhang Longxi, "The Critical Legacy of Oscar Wilde" 166).

When reviewing criticism against Wilde for his detachment from tradition and the classic, Zhang quotes Harold Bloom and Ellmann. Harold Bloom attacks Wilde because he is intimidated by the overwhelming influence (or rather threat) of the classic and tradition. Ellmann summarizes such ideas and suggests that "Wilde's mode was calculated juvenescence, and the characters in his books are always being warned by shrewder characters of the danger of listening to people older than themselves" (qtd. in Zhang Longxi, "The Critical Legacy of Oscar Wilde" 166). Zhang, however, disagrees with both scholars. Much as Wilde stresses the significance of creative criticism and opposes rigid attachment to the classic and tradition, he is not a defiant academic who fools around with word play without adequate cultivation, nor is he an irresponsible scholar whose work is reduced to only a "patchwork affair or a polished form of public entertainment" (Zhang Longxi, "The Critical Legacy of Oscar Wilde" 169). To Zhang, such criticism is unfair and reckless. Critics of Wilde, as Zhang argues, "forget their emphasis on the self-culture of the critic" (Ibid.). Zhang quotes Wilde's words, saying that "criticism demands infinitely more cultivation than creation does" (Ibid.). Opposing voices, as Zhang continues his rebuttal, fail to notice "his perfect sane and solid enumeration of the essentials of Shakespearean criticism, which includes practically everything a Shakespearean scholar should know" (Ibid.). Although Wilde disapproves of rigid adherence to the classic and tradition, he recognizes and emphasizes the cultivation that is necessary for qualified creativity and criticism. Scholars without nurture by the classic and tradition cannot afford creativity, and Wilde himself is a perfect model with remarkable erudition.

To Wilde, individual creativity is more important than and superior to "unity," which is reflected through the classic and tradition and should be attributed to creativity. "Unity is of the individual," but this does not mean that we should focus exclusively on creativeness and dispel unity. The two wrestle but are interdependent.

1.6　T. S. Eliot: Tradition and the Individual Talent

After the era of Enlightenment, when reason and science dominated, people shifted their focus from the supernatural and mysterious to the scientific and logical. People were no longer obsessed with tracing back to the superstitious; rather, they tried to reveal and disclose the reason and truth beneath the surface, which is regarded as a symbol of modernization. The discussion about the relationship between the classic and creativity also reflects such a transfer. T. S. Eliot (1888–1965), for example, uses a chemical reaction as a simile to illustrate how the classic and tradition interact and react with individual creativity. Scientific attitudes and rigorous logic have been adopted to clarify the paradoxical relationship between the classic and creativity. Compared to abstract and supernatural powers such as inspiration and genius, concepts such as the classic and tradition, which are understandable and accessible to human beings, have become the main targets to address. So, what is special about the concepts of *the classic* and *tradition*?

The *Oxford English Dictionary* defines *the classic* as literary works that are "of acknowledged excellence and/or importance."[1] They are "of the first class, of the highest rank or importance; constituting an acknowledged standard or model; of enduring interest and value."[2] From these two entries, we can derive several layers of meaning. Not only should its excellence and importance be widely approved and enjoy great popularity, but also its function to polish and regulate creativity as recognized standards should not be disgraced or disabled. Its popularity should not be temporal or instant, either.

The definitions of *tradition*, conversely, sound less descriptive than those of *the classic*. Rarely are there any acclaiming words that suggest its prestige in the entries. If the wide acknowledgement of a work that is part of *the classic* lies in its intrinsic excellence, *tradition* relies on what seems to be more grounding and touchable. One of the definitions suggests that *tradition* is "the body (or any one) of the experiences and usages of any branch or school of art or literature, handed down by predecessors and generally followed."[3] It is also "an embodiment of an old established custom or institution, a 'relic.'"[4] Although there are no acclaiming descriptions such as "excellence" or "acknowledgment," the definitions of *tradition* seem no less overwhelming. Unlike *the classic*, which dominates with an impressive excellence that prevails horizontally, *tradition* transcends vertically through time. It is empowered with the long-established consistence whose

---

[1] "classic, adj. and n." *OED Online*. Oxford University Press, December 2014. Web. 30 January 2015.

[2] Ibid.

[3] "Tradition, n." *OED Online*. Oxford University Press, December 2014. Web. 30 January 2015.

[4] Ibid.

accumulated strength through generations is hard to interrupt. Tradition therefore becomes irresistible, and to conform to tradition becomes an act that is obligatory, just as the definition suggests that it is "having almost the force of law."[1]

T. S. Eliot embraces such definitions of these two words. Two of his influential works, "What Is a Classic" and "Tradition and the Individual Talent" are indispensable references when we address questions about *the classic* and *tradition*. Eliot declares how significant the classic and tradition can be and shares his arguable yet sensible understanding of them within these two essays. Although he meant to counter the personal-feelings-oriented Romanticism, which, to him, is too subjective and indulges too much in personal emotions, he makes no negative statements about Romanticists' ideas. He merely emphasizes the significance of the classic and tradition, the value of which, from Eliot's perspective, is wrongly downgraded by the Romanticists.

To Eliot, the "acknowledged excellence and importance" suggested by the definition originates because of the inclusiveness of a classic. In "What Is a Classic," Eliot reminds us of the attributes that determine the value of the classic. They are "variety," "comprehensiveness," and "relatedness." First, the classic manages to appeal to scholars from diverse disciplines, whose specialized knowledge can always be nourished by reading the classic. "Variety," as Eliot elucidates, refers to the potential of the classic to be approached from interdisciplinary perspectives (Eliot, "What Is a Classic" 7). The classic should possess the quality to inspire intellectual minds from different specialized fields. Virgil's work, for example, is so inclusive that "no specialized knowledge or proficiency can confer the exclusive title to talk about Virgil" (Ibid.). Such inclusiveness not only breaks through the boundaries between different subjects but also encompasses individual specialties and preferences. As Eliot points out, "each can give his testimony of Virgil in relation to those subjects which he knows best, or upon which

---

[1] "Tradition, n." *OED Online*. Oxford University Press, December 2014. Web. 30 January 2015.

he has most deeply reflected" (Ibid.). Second, although the classic's sacredness makes it seemingly unapproachable, it can always synthesize with people's feelings and arouse empathy among them, in spite of their linguistic or cultural differences. The classic is not only academically inclusive but also emotionally comprehensive. The second attribute of the classic is "comprehensiveness." The classic works, as Eliot argues, "express the maximum possible of the whole range of feelings which represent the character of the people who speak that language" (Ibid. 27). The classic works "represent these at their best" and "have the widest appeal" (Ibid.). The classic is able to influence people's minds and resonate with their feelings, and it can arouse people's empathy regardless of their conditions and backgrounds. The third quality of the classic is "relatedness." The inclusiveness of the classic enables readers to broaden their cultural horizons. This goal cannot be achieved if people stay within their limited scope of knowledge that is derived from the same language or the same culture. The classic, as Eliot observes, reaches beyond the monolingual or intra-cultural environment. Being aware of the excellence of another culture and appreciating it will facilitate the progress and elevation of a civilization. Eliot suggests that "to make use of a foreign literature in this way marks a further stage of civilization beyond only making use of the earlier stages of one's own" (Ibid. 19). Virgil, as Eliot suggests, "was constantly adapting and using the discoveries, traditions and inventions of Greek poetry" (Ibid.), and "it is this development of one literature, or civilization, in relation to another, which gives a peculiar significance to the subject of Virgil's epic" (Ibid.). Being informed of the excellence of literature from another culture, masters are able to create the classic that can not only attract cross-cultural perspectives but also afford enduring discussions. Eliot declares that the classic affords cultural interaction not by merely adopting the literary elements of foreign cultures but because the classic arouses people's awareness of the "relatedness" of different cultures. It is more of a modest attitude to learn from each other, and it is the humble willingness to sacrifice and compromise during the interactions. It is only with all three of these features that the classic can gain prevailing approval. To Eliot, the classic is therefore academically, emotionally, and culturally inclusive.

The inclusiveness Eliot assigns to the classic, however, does not resemble what Hugo Meltzl intends to do when he includes multiple languages and topics. To encourage multiplicity and "polyglottism," Meltzl includes in his journal literature written in ten different languages concerning topics ranging from literary history to translation studies (Damrosch, "Hugo Meltzl" 15). Meltzl's idea of "inclusiveness" is to embrace differences. Eliot, conversely, suggests another kind of "inclusiveness." He advocates "a common style" that generalizes and summarizes individual differences. Eliot indicates the commonality of the style and refers to it as "a community of tastes." To Eliot, the inclusiveness of the classic alludes to the utmost inclusion of qualified tastes and deserved conventions of style. The classic must appeal to as many intelligent minds as possible that are capable of appreciating its excellence, and it includes all the merits that are supposed to have been embedded in a great literary work. The styles and the tastes that are reflected through the classic are widely acknowledged. Cultivation of these tastes and conventions is thus necessary and rewarding. It is important for us to acquire these so that we fit in and avoid eccentricity; however, any attempt to create eccentric or bizarre literary classics, as Eliot indicates, should be rightly condemned. We should not embrace any differences without evaluating them with the "common style," and we should not tolerate idiosyncrasy or "originality" that deviates from the "common taste." We may find that to include the more, the better does not count as what Eliot calls the inclusiveness of the classic, especially when we consider his remarks on the supremacy of English poetry and French prose (Eliot, "What Is a Classic" 13). The inclusiveness of the classic, to Eliot, is intended to select rather than to include.

To Eliot, the random and uncontrolled overflow of subjective emotions should not be counted as a reliable source or reasonable inspiration when poets produce great pieces of literature, nor should individuality and creativity be independent of cultivation and the classic. In fact, what individuality and creativity owe to the classic is so intrinsic and essential that it is hardly possible to escape from the classic's involvement. As Eliot implies, the "originality" that certain authors claim to acquire is only superficial and illusory. The influence received from the classic, conversely, is genetically inherited and, thus, unchangeable and undeniable. Eliot uses a metaphor to illustrate such an idea. He says that "in retrospect, we can see that he (the poet) is also the continuer of their traditions, that he preserves essential family characteristics, and that his different behavior is a difference in the circumstances of another age" (Ibid. 14). Ages when "originality" and "eccentricity" are valued, as Eliot furthers his argument, occur either before or after a classic age. Neither of them should be considered as "the golden age." Ages before the classic age did not accomplish adequate exploration of the language that affords deeper and dynamic development of the literature. Ages after the classic age, conversely, attempted in vain to surpass the classic age, the latter works of which had already exhausted the potential of the language (Ibid.).

Tradition, in Eliot's view, is even more "authoritarian" than the dictionary definition indicates. The power of it is more overwhelming than that of law. Rather than compelling and coercing people's behaviors, tradition influences and directs people's minds. Just like in the definition in the *Oxford English Dictionary*, tradition is the "body of experience and usages."[①] It is more of a material presence than a metaphysical existence. Tradition, as Eliot argues, constitutes the substance to be processed in the "chemical reaction" of literary creation. Without tradition, the substance, the chemical reaction, has nowhere to begin. Compared to tradition, individuality and subjectivity are reduced to only a "catalyst" in the "chemical reaction" of literary creation. The function of "the catalyst" cannot be fulfilled unless the substance is presented first. In his renowned work "Tradition and the Individual Talent," Eliot suggests that the process of creating poetry "takes place when a bit of finely filiated platinum is introduced into a chamber containing oxygen and sulphur dioxide" (Eliot, "Tradition" 30). The "bit of finely filiated platinum" thus refers to the individual creativity that participates in the process of literature production but does not necessarily determine or direct the process. Tradition, as Eliot explains, serves as the influential and enduring standard that measures and

---

① "Tradition, n." *OED Online.* Oxford University Press, December 2014. Web. 30 January 2015.

selects decedent literary works:

> No poet, no artist of any art, has his complete meaning alone. His significance, his appreciation is the appreciation of his relation to the dead poets and artists. You cannot value him alone; you must set him, for contrast and comparison, among the dead. (Ibid. 28)

Just as the simile of "catalyst" suggests, as strong as the personal emotions are, they are not truly involved with the creation of art, and, much as the individual talent overflows, it needs to conform to tradition. Excellence has already been defined by the classic. Rules have already been established by tradition. The classic and tradition, in this sense, have been endowed with supreme authority that can be neither overlooked nor denied.

It seems unfair to make individuality and creativity passively subject to the classic and tradition. The authority of the classic and tradition may be a heavy shackle, restraining any attempt to create anything significant outside its reigning domain. Individual creativity never seems to be able to escape being haunted by the "old fashions." Yet, as much as Eliot emphasizes the priority of the classic and tradition in literary creation, he never intends to completely remove individual creativity from the process of literary creation.

Instead, Eliot prefers a paradoxical yet reciprocal relationship between the classic and creativity, between tradition and individuality. In his article "Tradition and the Individual Talent," he suggests,

> The existing order is complete before the new work arrives; for order to persist after the supervention of novelty, the whole existing order must be, if so slightly altered; and so the relations, proportions, values of each work of art toward the whole are readjusted; and this is conformity between the old and the new. (Ibid.)

Tradition never denies contributions from individual creation. Rather, it communicates and relates to later and decedent works. The order established by tradition and the classic extends to later times and is the connection and bridge between the old and the new. Tradition and creativity witness a paradoxical interaction with each other.

In fact, although Eliot places much emphasis on the importance of the classic and tradition, his idea still resonates with what Plato, Pope, and Wordsworth advocate, as Eliot also recognizes how creativity participates in literary creation. These masters in Western literary history, as we can see from the above argument, all notice that both the classic and creativity are indispensable in the process of creating literature. They may have a different emphasis and focus when dealing with the paradoxical relationship between the two elements in literary creation, but neither of them makes the two mutually exclusive. What they advocate for is always a combination of the classic and creativity in literary creation. Eliot, for example, after explaining how important the classic and tradition are, summarizes his idea by drawing attention to "an unconscious balance" between the classic and creativity, tradition and originality:

> The persistence of literary creativeness in any people, accordingly, consists of the maintenance of an unconscious balance between tradition in the larger sense — the collective personality, so to speak, realized in the literature of the past — and the originality of the living generation. (Ibid. 15)

The feature of inclusiveness that Eliot detects in the classic alludes to "the collective personality." The classic cannot therefore be created without the contribution of personality and creativity. Individual creativeness in literature production relates to tradition and the classic so as to achieve a harmonious balance. The classic and tradition direct and nourish individual minds, while individual creativeness introduces freshness to the former. The communication between the classic and creativity is paradoxical and reciprocal at the same time.

1.7 Eliot Weinberger: Karmic Traces

T. S. Eliot, however, is not alone in giving priority to tradition and the classic in literary creation, nor are his insights too old or too conservative for contemporary minds to resonate with. Like T. S. Eliot, Eliot Weinberger

(1949–), in his book *Karmic Traces 1993–1999,* illustrates how the sense of past subtly yet inevitably influences the present. He prefaces the first article in the book, "Karmic Traces," with a passage adapted from Marcel Proust's *À la Recherche du Temps Perdu* (*In Search of Lost Time*) (Weinberger 141). The passage describes a scene where the author was reminded of his childhood when attracted by the smell of a dessert (Ibid.). Weinberger uses the metaphor of scent to convey the idea of "karmic traces." The traces enable transmission and inheritance that transcend time and space and that remind and resonate.

The phenomenon of "karmic traces" also occurs when it comes to literature and literary creation. The classic and tradition travel through time and history. They overcome the threat of becoming obsolete and outdated, and their value and meaning are not jeopardized by the longevity of time. Weinberger first admits the validity of contextualizing poems within a specific historical background. He suggests that "a poem belongs to a historical moment, fixed by time and place, most evident in the language the poem speaks, but also in its range of concerns and the form — its clothes of fashion — in which the poem is wrapped" (Ibid. 147); however, he immediately reminds us that poetry "simultaneously exists outside of the historical continuum" (Ibid.):

> Ancient poems, the great ones, are as immediate, or more immediate, than those written yesterday. Some indefinable living matter in the poem — perhaps it is its karmic traces — allows it to remain vital as it persists through the ages, ever as the language in which it was written dies out, even as it travels by translation from language to language. (Ibid.)

To Weinberger, the capability of poems to transcend time and space is never inferior to that of memory or dreams. By detaching poetry from its "history continuum," Weinberger frees poetry from what is shackled by particular poets, time, or language. Weinberger elevates the classic and tradition to the level where they have a metaphysical existence, like "karmic traces," that can, regardless of external changes, "remain vital as [they persist] through ages" (Ibid.). They will never be devalued or deteriorated over time and history. The greater the classic and tradition, the fresher they become along the time continuum. The development of the classic and tradition can be independent of the specific restraints of time and place. The classic and tradition can transcend time, and they can reach across linguistic and cultural borders.

The impact of the classic and tradition on literature development is not weakened as time passes. The classic always manages to unconsciously and miraculously influence the minds of decedent generations of literature, and individual creativity can always become transcendentally connected and related to the past. To depict such a mysterious phenomenon, Weinberger quotes words from an ancient Chinese literary critic:

> Yeh Hsieh, in his treatise *The Origin of Poetry*, comments: "When what I write is the same as what a former master wrote, it means that we were one in our reflections. And when I write something different from former masters, I may be filling in something missing from their work. Or it is possible that the former masters are filling in something missing in my work." (Ibid. 150)

The Chinese poem is therefore "filled with skillful allusions to other poems, [and] was seen as one more piece in an unending dialogue between the living and the dead" (Ibid.). Assisted by such a transcendental feature, the classic and traditional poems manage to nourish and participate in the literary creations of later times. Such an uninterruptable correspondence between the old and the new encourages Weinberger to consciously imitate Jane Austen's renowned statement in *Pride and Prejudice* and to assume that "it is nearly a universal belief, among poets, that someone else writes what they write" (Ibid. 154).

Yet, much as Weinberger vividly depicts how the classic and tradition irreducibly transcend to the present, he does not deny the function and participation of individual creativity of the living generation. Like Plato, Pope, Wilde, and Eliot, Weinberger suggests that the two enjoy a reciprocal relationship. Individual creativity has a positive function. Weinberger suggests that in the West, "tradition means that the living modify the dead" (Ibid. 151). The living generation, with the originality of the times, contributes to the renewal and adaptation of the classic and tradition within new eras and environments. Weinberger also suggests that "in China, one might say that the dead revise their own poems through the living" and that "in Chinese poetry, the tradition meant transmission: continual change in a past that was moving steadily forward" (Ibid.). This reminds us of Eliot when he suggests that individual creativity serves as a stimulant in the process of literary creation. The originality of the living generation motivates the classic and tradition to improve. In addition, like Eliot, who reveals a kind of established yet changeable order for the new individuality to conform to, Weinberger recognizes the "transmission" from tradition to new creativity. The classic and tradition are not stagnant; they themselves are constantly experiencing changes. The creativeness of individuals does not need to rigidly conform to the classic and tradition; rather, the two rely on each other for mutual benefit. The classic and tradition transcend time to cultivate fresh minds, and courtesy of the introduction of the new creativity in the system of literature development, the classic and tradition enjoy a "continual change in a past that was moving steadily forward."

As we move along literary history, we find that, concerning the question about the relationship between the classic and creativity, great minds think alike. Their ideas and discussions resonate with one another. They all recognize and endorse the paradoxical relationship between the classic and creativity. They all avoid dichotomizing the two, and they all strive to describe the interactions between the two. The prestige and impact of the classic and tradition may be overwhelming and threatening to individual creativity, but the classic and tradition are indispensable in modifying and directing individual creativity. Individual creativity may be immature and uncontrollable, but it motivates the classic and tradition to change and improve. Plato's poetry and inspiration, Pope's Nature and Homer, Wilde's unity and individual, Eliot's tradition and individual talent, and Weinberger's karmic traces all prove the interdependent and mutually beneficial relationship between the classic and creativity.

In fact, the consistency in thought about the classic and creativity is not only reflected within a single cultural context. The same cultural cultivation can surely prompt similar thinking and reasoning; however, we can also find affinities in thought when it comes to comparing different cultural contexts concerning the question of the classic and creativity. Just as Weinberger suggests that karmic traces enable classic poetry to transcend time differences and linguistic borders, discussions about the relationship between the classic and creativity always resonate with one another, regardless of geographical borders or cultural differences.

Chapter Two

The Classic and Creativity in
Chinese Literary Criticism

The geographical distance between the East and the West has not distanced the ideas of the two sides. In fact, geographical position is merely a relative term. Two places, however close they are, can be taken as extremes in two contrasting directions. Conversely, two places that suffer from a long commute can still be connected with each other.

Efforts to isolate and dichotomize Chinese culture from the Western world seem to have been consistently yet unreasonably made. Hegel (1770–1831), for example, in his *Science of Logic,* suggests that the Chinese language is inferior in the sense that it lacks logic of thought:

> It is to the advantage of a language when it possesses a wealth of logical expressions, that is, distinctive expressions specifically set aside for thought determinations. Many of the prepositions and articles already pertain to relations based on thought (in this the Chinese language has apparently not advanced that far culturally, or at least not far enough). (Hegel 12)

Although given in parentheses, Hegel's sense of superiority over the Chinese language is no less obvious. Another "advance" in German language, as Hegel proceeds with his argument, is that dialectical thinking is revealed in the use of the language:

> The German *aufheben* ("to sublate" in English) has a twofold meaning in the language: it equally means "to keep," "to 'preserve'" and "to cause to cease," "to put an end to." ... It must strike one as remarkable that a language has come to use one and the same word

for two opposite meanings. For speculative thought it is gratifying to find words that have in themselves a speculative meaning. (Ibid. 81–82)

In his article "The 'Tao' and the 'Logos': Notes on Derrida's Critique of Logocentrism," Zhang Longxi argues against such cultural and linguistic superiority. He takes the concept of *Yi* (易) in Chinese culture and literature, which also contains two paradoxical meanings: "conciseness" and "change" or "constancy" as an example. Such "dialectic reciprocity of opposite terms," as Zhang argues, "is a theme overly reiterated in ancient Chinese writing" (Zhang Longxi, "The 'Tao' and the 'Logos'" 386). Yet these affinities have been discredited by Hegel and downgraded by him as "primitive dialectics, abstract, superficial, always going round in a circle of immobilism, exteriority, and naturality" (Ibid.).

To revise such prejudiced and unreasonable views is urgent and necessary, and attracting more readers of Chinese literature will facilitate greater familiarity with Chinese culture and thereby preclude uninformed misunderstandings and deliberate misinterpretation.

Dialectical thinking, for example, is not only reflected through words in the Chinese language but is also revealed through literary criticism throughout Chinese history. Discussions about the question of the relationship between the classic and creativity, for example, overcome these fabricated differences and connect different cultures with unexpected affinities. Like the paradoxical relationship between the classic and creativity indicated by the discussion about it across time and history in the Western world, the contrasting and complementary interactions between the classic and creativity are also evinced by discussions about it throughout China's history of literary criticism.

2.1 *The Book of Poetry* and the "Mao" Preface: Emotion and Old Custom

The Book of Poetry is the earliest collection of poems that were created from 1100 BCE to 600 BCE. The poems in the collection rhyme and are melodious, expressing basic and primitive feelings and ideas. The simplicity however, has attracted consistent academic interest. The "Mao" preface, for example, was attached to the collections during the Han Dynasty. It even develops into a school of criticism in studies of *The Book of Poetry*. In the preface, which was created early in Chinese literary history, we can already find an analysis of the paradoxical relationship between the classic and creativity in poetry creation.

As the preface suggests, the poems were produced to express the will in individual minds and were inspired by personal feelings and emotions. Poetry arises from within, where the inner voices can be so strong that words with rhythmic features cannot express it to the utmost but body gestures are needed to accompany the melodious poems:

> The Ode is where the aim [*zhi*] goes. While in the heart [*xin*], it is the aim; manifested in words, it is an Ode. Emotion [*qing*] moves within and takes shape in words. Words are not enough, and so one sighs it. Sighing it is not enough, and so one draws it out in song. Drawing it out in song is not enough, and so all unawares one's hands dance it and one's feet tap it out. (Zoeren 95)

To follow one's aim and will in poetry creation is to internalize the origin of poetry. It seems that poetry creation resonates with personal minds and individual creativity more than it resonates with cultivation or custom. The process of poetry creation begins within an individual's mind. Feelings are prompted before words are expressed, and words are merely the form that carries the utterance of mind.

Although the preface illuminates that poetry originates from personal feelings and emotions, it does not deny the effects of tradition and customs that are received externally:

> "Air" [*feng*] means "suasion" [*feng*]; it means "teaching." Suasion is exerted in order to move [one's prince?], and teaching aims to transform [the people]. (Ibid.)

Poems under *feng* are mostly written from the perspective of common people and individuals. Themes in the poems range from love between men and women and attachment between parents and children to hatred of the cruelty of life and admiration of beauty. These would all seem to be simple and ordinary topics without any intended moral teaching or connotation; however, as the preface suggests, poems of *feng* intend to teach and transform people. They exert an impact on the people who read them: They cultivate their minds with the right lessons and direct them in the right way. In this sense, the poems themselves function as the classic and tradition. In fact, *The Book of Poetry* is indeed an essential part of the Chinese classics. The popularity and readership of *The Book of Poetry* has not deteriorated over the centuries, nor has its authority as a literary masterpiece been challenged by different political regimes throughout history. It remains indispensable in contemporary times for cultivation in Chinese literature and culture, not only in the realm of academia but also among common people. *The Book of Poetry* is never removed from teaching materials in China. Even pupils at elementary schools can now recite these poems.

Aside from functioning as the classic and tradition, *The Book of Poetry*, although, as the preface suggests, is derived from personal feelings and emotions, it is still regulated by custom and tradition, and it still traces back to the old and inherits the old:

> Emotion is manifested in the voice. When the voice is patterned [*cheng wen*] we call it tone [*yin*]. They knew how things had changed and longed for the old customs. So the Changed Airs derive from feelings and yet stop within [the bounds of] ritual and righteousness. That they derive from feelings is because that's how people are. That they stop within ritual and rightness is all due to the beneficence [*ze*] of the early kings. (Ibid. 96)

According to the above passage, then, to express feelings and emotions is not the ultimate goal of poetry; rather, poetry is produced to convey a sense of nostalgia for the "old custom" and to voice people's desire to relate to the tradition and to restore it. Feelings and emotions are not to be expressed wildly without any control; rather, they are regulated and refined by "ritual and rightness." The individual creativity is not completely subjective and determined by the individual himself; rather, it still yields to boundaries. The individual creativity is just relatively free. Although what shackles individual creativity here is more in a political sense than in a classical or traditional sense, its function and impacts on individual creativity are similar and correspondent.

Zhu Xi (1130–1200), however, disagrees with such influences of moral teaching on the poems and of the poems in *The Book of Poetry*. Zhu Xi is also a literary critic who is renowned in Chinese literary history. Zhang Longxi, in his book *Allegoresis: Reading Canonical Literature East and West,* quotes Zhu Xi to explain how Zhu "dismissed conventional readings at his time that ignored the integrity of the canonical text and its literal sense" (137):

> They force the text by tortuous means to comply with the preface and even willingly sacrifice the poet's original intention with no scruples. That is the great damage the preface brings about ... I interpreted the poems solely according to the prefaces without considering the meaning of the poems in their own context, then I would have wronged the sages themselves. (qtd. in Zhang Longxi, *Allegoresis* 137)

Zhu refuses to refer to the preface to facilitate his interpretation of the poems in *The Book of Poetry*; rather, he abuses the misleading effect caused by it. The reason why Zhu considers the preface misleading is that it politicizes the interpretations of the poems. When explaining how the personal feelings and emotions are restricted, the preface takes the "ritual and rightness is all due to the beneficence [ze] of the early kings" as standards and measures to evaluate and regulate individual feelings and creativity. At the same time, although Zhu disagrees with the influence of the old, he must agree with the preface in the sense that it suggests that the poems derive from personal feelings and emotions. Zhu argues that poetry is "the excess of language in which the mind formulates what the heart feels when affected by things" (Ibid.). Zhu similarly emphasizes the individual element that determines the creation of poems in *The Book of Poetry*.

Therefore, we can see that the paradoxical relationship between individual creativity and the old custom was already touched upon at this early age in Chinese literature studies. In fact, discussions like this have been enduringly and consistently given through Chinese literary history. Regardless of the difference in time, the correspondence in ideas can always be detected.

2.2   Lu Ji and *Wen Fu*: Feeling, Intent, and Ancient Canons

Another Chinese literary critic, Lu Ji (or Lu Chi, 261–303) also discusses the origin of literary creation in his work *Wen Fu*, which is not only renowned in its domestic culture, Chinese literature and culture, but also attracts attention overseas. Several versions of its translation into English have appeared in academia in the Western world. The translation of the title of the article, for example, already has four versions: *The Poetic Exposition on Literature* by Stephen Owen, *Wen Fu* by Sam Hamill, *Essay on Literature* by Shih-Hsiang Chen, and *Rhymeprose on Literature* by Achilles Fang. Lu Ji's ingenious insight resonates with diverse cultures.

At the beginning of *Wen Fu,* Lu Ji describes how he is inspired by the excellence of masterpieces from the past and praises the enlightening classic and tradition. We can derive such an idea from Stephen Owen's and Sam Hamill's translations of the first few lines of *Wen Fu*:

> He stands in the very center, observes in the darkness,
> Nourishes feeling and intent in the ancient canons.
> ...
> He sings of the blazing splendor of moral power inherited by this age,
> Chants of the pure fragrance (or "reputation") of predecessors,
> Roams in the groves and treasure houses of literary works,
> Admires the perfect balance of their intricate and lovely craft.
> With strong feeling he puts aside the book and takes his writing brush
> To make it manifest in literature. (Owen, *Readings in Chinese Literary Thought* 87, 92)

> The poet stands at the center
> of a universe,
> contemplating the enigma,
> drawing sustenance
> from masterpieces of the past

...
Learn to recite the classics;
sing in the clear virtue
of ancient masters.
Explore the treasures of the classics
where form and content are born.
Thus moved, I lay aside my books
and take writing brush in hand
to compose this poem. (Lu 6–7)

Lu Ji attaches importance to the works of predecessors. Individual "intent" and "feeling" are "nourished" by and "draw sustenance" from the "treasures" and "intricate craft" of the classic and tradition. The resonation with the predecessors' minds is so perceived by individuals and the excellence of the masterpieces from the past is so inspiring that he has to release and ease his strong feelings by introducing the resonation and the excellence into his own writing. According to Hamill's translation, Lu Ji even attributes the development of literature's "content and form" to the classic and tradition.

Indeed, Lu Ji highly praises the positive function that the classic and tradition perform in the process of literary creation. At the same time, however, Lu Ji also emphasizes the significance of individual creativity. Although Lu Ji pays respect to the classic and tradition, he also urges poets to break the shackles of old customs and to pursue what has not been achieved. Rigid conformity and repetition are to be avoided. Inspiring imagination and creativity are to be advocated. Poets should be "buds" that aspire to blossom rather than flowers that have already blossomed and are destined for peril:

He gathers in writing omitted by a hundred generations,
Pick rhymes neglected for a thousand years;
It falls away — that splendid flowering of dawn, already unfurled,
But there opens the unblown budding of evening. (Owen, *Readings in Chinese Literary Thought* 102)

Like Plato, Lu Ji touches on the concept of "inspiration" in the process of creating poetry. He also attributes the production of literature to a stream of unconscious power that is derived from a supernatural place beyond humans' grasp. Its coming and going is not to be controlled by human beings but is attributed to a kind of "Heaven's motive impulses":

> At the conjunction of stirring and response,
> At the demarcation between blockage and passage,
> What comes cannot be halted,
> What goes off cannot be stopped.
> When it hides, it is like a shadow disappearing,
> When it moves, it is like an echo rising.
> When Heaven's motive impulses move swiftly on the best course,
> What confusion is there that cannot be put in order? (Ibid. 173–175)

To value individual creativity and inspiration, as some scholars interpret, is an encouraging gesture, considering the context of Lu Ji's time. Hamill, in his introduction to his translation of *Wen Fu,* suggests that in Lu Ji's time, the cultivation of the classic and tradition is required for "an educated man" (Lu xxiii). Scholars highly respect the "five cartloads" of the classic and tradition, and they have been protective of their "irreplaceable scrolls" (Ibid.). With such a serious sense of the classic and tradition, scholars elevate the classic and tradition to a supreme level.

"To this seriousness," Hamill argues, "Lu adds a *hsin*, or 'heart/mind,' which is unifying" (Ibid.). To Hamill, such a gesture unifies "emotion and reason" (Ibid.). It helps poets to achieve a positive balance between the two and to acquire a "fully integrated personality" (Ibid.). To shift the focus from tradition and the classic to individual feelings and creativity in literary creation, to Hamill, is an innovating gesture.

Interestingly, contrary to Hamill, some scholars assert that to attach importance to the classic and tradition is a breakthrough. Zhang Huaijin, in his preface to *Wen Fu,* [1] suggests that Lu Ji detaches individual intent and feeling from the subjectivity of human beings and rather attaches it to the

---

[1] This book is in Chinese. The quotation from this book is translated by the author.

classic and tradition. This is the new contribution made by Lu Ji in *Wen Fu*. To Zhang, the intent and feeling that is expressed through poetry owes more to the cultivation of the classic and tradition. It does not arise from one's own mind, independently of nurture or education. Feeling and intent, like what Lu Ji suggests in *Wen Fu*, are prompted and motivated by the excellence of masterpieces from the past rather than generated with no stimulant in one's mind:

> The contribution of *Wen Fu* lies in its development of the aesthetic idea about "Poetry expresses will." "Nourishes feeling and intent in the ancient canons," here to put "feeling and intent" together is not a simple combination of words but is a relation between content; and feeling and intent has been detached from subjective minds and shifted to "ancient canons." This adds new elements (to literary creation), which shows a sense of innovation (Zhang Huaijin 7).

In fact, both Hamill and Zhang Huaijin adopt a biased and incomprehensive perspective when analyzing Lu Ji's *Wen Fu*. They only detect one aspect that is revealed in Lu Ji's *Wen Fu*. "Feeling and intent" and "ancient canons," "Heaven's motive impulses," and "intricate and lovely craft" of the masterpieces from the past all participate in the creation of literature. Lu Ji makes a solid and comprehensive argument in *Wen Fu*. He notices the contrasting yet complementary relationship between the classic and creativity in this famous article, but he does not take a biased perspective. This is why the article resonates with so many readers.

2.3   Liu Xie: Poetry Means Disciplined Human Emotion

Liu Xie (or Liu Hsieh, 465–520) expresses similar ideas. The fame of Liu Xie as a famous Chinese literary critic in ancient times was established and enhanced by his renowned work *The Literary Mind and the Carving of Dragons (Wen Xin Diao Long)*. Like Lu Ji, Liu Xie notices the supernatural power that

48 influences and participates in literary creation. To him, the respectable status of literature is bestowed and guaranteed by the supreme and primitive power of "Heaven and Earth." The sentences with which Liu Xie opens the book are *"Wen*, or pattern, is a very great power indeed" and "It is born with Heaven and Earth" (Liu 8). Liu Xie traces the origin of literature to the very start of the universe. It will resemble Heaven and Earth in the sense of eternity and fundamentality. Symbolized by such authorities that are not accessible or alterable by human efforts, literary creation finds a shrine to rest in, which not only ensures its consistent survival throughout history and time but also enhances its prestige.

Liu Xie also emphasizes the importance of the classic and tradition. There is one special part, entitled "The Classics as Literary Sources," in *The Literary Mind and the Carving of Dragons* that contributes to illustrating why the classics are significant. In this part, Liu Xie reviews in detail the essential lessons given by each representative classic work in Chinese literature: *The Book of Changes*, *The Book of Poetry*, *The Book of Rites*, and *The Spring and Autumn*. From these classics, people are able to access "principles which are absolute in regard to human nature and emotions" (Ibid. 17). Readers can also be nurtured with advanced linguistic skills and language sense, as in the classic, there is "language which conforms to the best literary principles" (Ibid.). By cultivating the classic, people are educated with "proper principles," and "their 'light shines far and wide'" (Ibid. 18).

Again, like Lu Ji, Liu Xie not only insists on the classic's function in literary creation, but he also notices how individual creativity and emotion stimulate literature production. Liu Xie begins his argument by quoting Great Shun's words that "poetry is the expression of sentiments, and songs are these expressions set to music" to support his hypothesis. He then proceeds with his argument by analyzing how individual emotion is transformed into poetry. He suggests that "that which is the sentiment within the mind becomes poetry when expressed in words. It is here indeed that literary form unfurls itself to communicate reality" (Ibid. 31–32). Yet, while confirming the positive effect exerted by individual emotion on poetry creation, Liu Xie furthers his argument by suggesting that the subjective feeling and individual emotion should be regulated and refined in poetry, which is actually "disciplined human emotion":

> Poetry means discipline, disciplined human emotion. The single idea that runs through the three hundred poems in the *Book of Poetry* is freedom from undisciplined thought. The interpretation of poetry as disciplined human emotions is in thorough agreement with this observation. (Ibid. 32)

In fact, the argument that poetry disciplines individual emotion resembles the function that is performed by the classic in terms of creativity. Cultivated by the classic and tradition, poets are more skilled and more fluent in expressing their feelings in a delicate and refined way. In Liu Xie's argument, the classic and individual feeling therefore strike a harmonious balance in the process of creating poetry and literature. Neither of them is removable from the process. Such ideas not only resonate with those of his predecessors, but they are also inherited by literary critics later than Liu Xie.

2.4 Yan Yu: Judgment and Spontaneous Enlightenment

The appeal for poets to cultivate themselves with the classic and tradition and to acquire proper judgment and a taste of art is also voiced by Yan Yu, a literary critic who lived around the twelfth century in China. He initiates his persuasion in *T'sang Lang's Remarks on Poetry* by encouraging poets to make *shi* (识) the indispensable priority when creating poetry. Stephen Owen, translates *shi* as "judgment" (Owen, *Readings on Chinese Literary Thought* 394). *Shi*, as Yan Yu proceeds with his argument, turns out to be a poet's acquaintance with poems created during the dynasties of Han, Wei, Jin, and High Tang (Ibid.). It also includes his or her acknowledgment of their significance, his or her ability to appreciate the excellence, and his or her willingness to abide by the standards of excellence. The classic and tradition from these periods can assist poets in cultivating better judgment and a better taste of poetry writing. Yan

50 suggests that "judgment is the dominant factor in the study of poetry. The beginning must be correct, and your mind must be set on the highest goals" (qtd. in Owen, *Readings on Chinese Literary Thought* 394). To achieve these goals, as Yan advises, poets should "take for [their] teacher the poetry of the Han, Wei, and High T'ang" (Ibid.). Poets who ignore or downgrade such excellence and who retreat from it are considered less determined and will be derailed in their pursuit of literary achievement. Just as Yan argues, poets should be directed to the proper and "correct beginning" and should be assigned with the "highest goals"; otherwise, "the vilest poetry demon will enter [their] breast" (Ibid.). The significance of the correct cultivation of the classic and tradition is supreme. As Yan asserts, "if you haven't yet reached your goals, you can always try harder; but if you err in your direction at the beginning, the more you rush on, the farther you will get off course. This will be because your beginnings were not correct" (Ibid. 394–395). The classic and tradition guide poets on their way. Being educated in the classic and tradition and being familiar with it, poets can establish solid knowledge upon which they can make better judgments, acquire better tastes, and express their own ideas more effectively and more easily.

At the same time, Yan Yu also notices something other than the classic and tradition that functions and participates in the creation of poetry. Yan Yu indicates that "poetry involves a distinct material that has nothing to do with books" and that "poetry involves a distinct interest that has nothing to do with a natural principle" (Ibid. 406). He notices how the counterparts of the conscious cultivation of the classic and tradition, the spontaneous feelings and unconscious inspiration that arise from an individual's inner mind and supernatural power, assist poets in achieving a higher level of literature production; however, he does not deny the positive function of the classic and tradition, as he suggests, "Still, if you don't read extensively and learn all there is to know about natural principle, you can't reach the highest level" (Ibid.). Yet Yan Yu immediately adds to the above statement by saying, "But the very best involves what is known as 'not getting onto the road of natural principle' and 'not falling into the trap of words'" (Ibid.).

To explain how innate feeling stimulates poetry writing, Yan Yu, like Lu Ji and Liu Xie, quotes the "Mao" preface to *The Book of Poetry*, which states that "poetry is 'to sing what is in the heart'" (Ibid.). Such individual emotion and intent, however, are not deliberately perceived; rather, as Yan Yu indicates, they are unconscious and spontaneous, and they are more like the untouchable and untraceable inspiration mentioned by Plato. Yan Yu uses a metaphor to illustrate this feature. He suggests,

> In the stirring and excitement of their poetry, the High T'ang writers were those antelopes that hang by their horns, leaving no tracks to be followed. Where they are subtle, there is a limpid and sparkling quality that can never be quite fixed and determined. (Ibid.).

In fact, to achieve such unconscious enlightenment is the supreme goal for Yan Yu, compared to which the cultivation of the classic and tradition is merely secondary. The classic and tradition, as Yan Yu indicates, if detached from the supreme goal of acquiring the enlightenment, can even be abandoned. Stephen Owen, for example, detects such a sense conveyed by Yan Yu. Owen suggests that "in his own program for the 'study of poetry' Yan Yu cannot entirely abandon Sung bookishness; but he transforms it, intensifies it, and then transcends it. For him, earlier poetry and its books are loved and resented, necessary and unnecessary" (Owen, *Readings on Chinese Literary Thought* 410). Such an observation reveals the paradoxical feature of the classic and tradition. It is the foundation upon which we achieve the enlightening moment, but it is only the foundation, which is beneath and inferior to the supreme goal. Owen proceeds with his argument by referring to Yan Yu's instruction to his students. According to Yan Yu, they should "begin with an intensive course of reading" (qtd. in Owen, *Readings on Chinese Literary Thought* 410). Yet Owen immediately adds, "But this is a course of study that is ultimately supposed to take the student beyond study — the moment of enlightenment in which the possibility of true poetry first appears" (Owen, *Readings on Chinese Literary Thought* 410). Yan Yu's idea, as Owen summarizes, is therefore that "'spontaneous enlightenment' is the end of a course of study" (Ibid. 399).

What Yan Yu here strives to pursue and accomplish highly resembles the concept of "inspiration" in Plato's discussion about the relationship between poetry and inspiration. Owen defines the goal as "spontaneous enlightenment" (Ibid.). Like inspiration, "spontaneous enlightenment" is beyond human understanding and grasp because "it is not an act of will, nor can it be willed: it can only be prepared for" (Ibid.). It is also related to supernatural and sacred origins, as it corresponds with the word *divinity* (Ibid.).

Yan Yu's idea therefore resonates with the ideas of Liu Xie and Lu Ji in the sense that they all notice the paradoxical relationship between the classic and individual creativity. Although Yan Yu prioritizes "spontaneous enlightenment" over the cultivation of the classic and tradition, he still acknowledges the directing and grounding function of the classic and tradition. Just as Owen suggests when he tries to define the word *enlightenment*, which is the most deserving goal from Yan Yu's perspective, "enlightenment means many things, but in Yan Yu's case it is primarily a unity of knowing and being" (Ibid.). "Knowing" refers to the sense that one acquires knowledge of the classic and tradition so as to cultivate oneself with proper judgment and better tastes. The gesture to obtain knowledge then becomes the state of acquiring knowledge; thus, "knowing" transforms into "being." With such a transformation completed, one is prepared when the enlightening moment comes.

2.5   Yuan Mei: Heart and Hand

Yuan Mei (1716–1797), an eighteenth-century poet and literary critic, emphasizes the importance of individual creativity and emotion in writing poetry. Contrary to the main stream of thinking in his time, which prioritized references to past masterpieces in one's work, Yuan Mei's idea encourages people to shatter the shackles of the classic and tradition from the past. The counterparts, as Yuan Mei defines them, are "heart" and "hand," with the former embodying individuality and the latter reflecting the collective past. The heart should direct and dominate the hand rather than the other way around. Arthur Waley (1889–1966), for example, translated a passage from Yuan Mei's *Sui Yuan Shi Hua* (*Sui Yuan Poetry Talk*), in which Yuan criticizes the irresponsible assimilation of individual work in the past and the complete dependence on the classic and tradition:

> P'u Hsien said: "Poetry is born in the heart and made by the hand. If it is the heart that controls the hand, then all is well; but if the hand does the heart's work, all is lost. Today those who make imitation the basis of poet help themselves by taking a bit here and a bit there, all of it raked out of piles of old paper, instead of relying on what flows from their own feelings. That is what I call 'the hand doing the heart's work.'" (Waley 173)

Waley, in his book *Yuan Mei: Eighteenth Century Chinese Poet,* suggests that a "close imitation of some approved ancient period or individual great master" is rightly condemned in the process of literary creation (Ibid. 167). In Yuan Mei's time, it seems to have become a custom and priority of scholars to borrow "phrases and even whole lines from the great writers of the past"; however, to Waley, such a gesture cannot result in the achievement of great masterpieces (Ibid.). To Waley, what Yuan Mei advocates and maintains is "an expression of individual temperament and feeling" (Ibid.). The scope of the classic and the realm of tradition from the past cannot be regarded as restraints or regulations to be conformed to, but poets should "find [their] own phrasing, [their] own idiom ... within the general framework of traditional techniques" (Ibid.).

Although Yuan Mei emphasizes the importance of producing works that have an individual style and that express personal feeling and emotion, he does not appeal to poets to completely abandon the collective past. Yuan quotes another poet and suggests that "it is most important for poets to do a lot of reading" (qtd. in Waley 172), but he immediately adds that "this is only as a refreshment of the spirit" (Ibid.). Instead of removing traces of the classic and tradition from individual works, poets should conceal the sense of past beneath their personal style in their individual works. To Yuan, instead of showing off their erudition and cultivation, poets should embed the sense of past and the classic into and behind individual creativity and personal feeling.

As Yuan explains, "if neither the poet himself nor the reader knows exactly how this book-learning has affected a poem, then it is a true poem. But if he tries to deliberately dazzle us by the range of his reading, then at once he falls into an inferior category" (Ibid.).

It seems that Yuan Mei prefers individual temperament and personal feeling to the classic and tradition in poetry creation. Yet some scholars argue that Yuan Mei also recognizes the significance of the past. Unlike some ancient critics, who only acknowledge the supreme function of "inspiration" and "disposition" in the process of creating poetry, Yuan Mei suggests a combination of "learning from the past" and "listening to the heart." Zhang Shaokang, in his book *Zhong Guo Wen Xue Li Lun Pi Ping Jian Shi* (*Brief History of Chinese Literary Theory and Criticism*),[1] quotes several of Yuan Mei's works to support such an idea. In his *Xu Shi Pin* (*To Continue the Talk About Poetry*), Yuan Mei suggests that "if we do not learn from predecessors, we have nothing to follow. But if we completely resemble the past, where can we put our own ideas?" (qtd. in Zhang Shaokang 363). In his *Bo Xi* (*Extensive Learning*), Yuan Mei argues that "if words are not derived from learning, they are not authorized voices" (Ibid.). In his most renowned work, *Sui Yuan Shi Hua*, Yuan Mei admits that, although the inspiration and disposition dominate the process of literary creation, "if human efforts have not achieved the utmost, the inspiration has no reason to come" (Ibid.). He proceeds with this argument by asserting that "although we emphasize the importance of inspiration, it still requires human efforts to acquire it" (Ibid.). In the same book, Yuan Mei coins a fascinating and vivid metaphor to elaborate on the relationship between inborn inspiration and acquired cultivation. Yuan compares the expression of individual creativity and personal disposition to the delicate skin and charismatic smile of a beauty (Zhang Shaokang 364). Quotations and references to the past, conversely, are like the clothes and accessories that are acquired after birth (Ibid.). To be a truly pretty beauty, one needs to rely on both the inherited features of

[1] This book is written in Chinese. Quotations from this book are translated by the author.

appearance and acquired outfits.

Thus, although Yuan Mei is regarded as a representative of the school of criticism that emphasizes the importance of individual inspiration and disposition, he still acknowledges the indispensable function performed by the classic and tradition. By bearing a sense of the past in mind, as Yuan explains, poets can grasp the inspiration and refine their personal disposition for expression in poetry.

2.6   Qian Zhongshu: Emotion and Talent, Nature, and Art

Qian Zhongshu (1910–1998) can be regarded as the most erudite scholar in both Chinese literature and Western literature. His wide area of expertise and solid mastery of knowledge enable him to adopt comprehensive perspectives and to provide a convincing argument either when he horizontally compares cultures across geographical borders or when he vertically traces along the history continuum. Concerning the paradoxical relationship between the classic and creativity, Qian is certainly qualified to review discussions about it and to summarize and extract ideas from them.

In his book *Tan Yi Lu (Talks About Art)*[1], Qian creates an independent chapter, "Emotion and Talent," which talks about the relationship between individual emotion and cultivation. He begins his argument by quoting Wang Ji's (with unknown birth and death date, who lived in sometime during 265–317) words that "literature derives from emotion" (Qian 39). Unlike Lu Ji, Liu Xie, or Yan Yu, Qian Zhongshu does not quote the most familiarized source of origin of this statement, *The Book of Poetry*, but refers to Wang Ji, a less well-known but more legendary figure in Chinese literary history. He lived during the Xijin Dynasty and was not only prominent in

---

[1]   This book is written in Chinese. Quotations from the book are translated by the author.

literature studies but was also appointed as general of the court in his time. To quote Wang Ji not only shows how well-read Qian is, but it also reveals the prevalence of the statement that emotion is the origin of poetry.

56

Yet Qian immediately rebuts such a claim by saying that, although literature originates because of emotion, "emotion is not poetry" (Ibid.). Qian emphasizes this argument by repeating that "emotion facilitates poetry creation, but emotion is not poetry" (Ibid. 40). To Qian, poetry is more "art" (艺) than "emotion" (情) (Ibid.). Art, as Qian proceeds with his argument, must have "rules" and "taboos"; it is thus "discipline" (持) (Ibid.). This resonates with Liu Xie's comments in *The Literary Mind and the Carving of Dragons: The Book of Poetry,* which is always held as a work that embodies human emotion and innate nature, rather reflects how individual emotion is disciplined and regulated and then properly expressed. Qian embraces the same ideas. He argues that "to discipline one's emotion can enable one to create poetry" (Ibid.). In fact, the function of art, in Qian's words, resembles that of "technique." It has rules to be followed, and it is to be acquired and cultivated. Qian seems to emphasize the importance of being educated by the classic and tradition apart from the commonly assumed element of poetry, human emotion.

Yet, following the above argument, Qian proposes another concept: "talent" (才) (Ibid.). As Qian asserts, "talent" determines whether art can be applied successfully (Ibid.). To support this idea, he quotes several poets in Chinese literary history. Yan Huangmen (531–595) suggests that if you are not a genius, you should not forcibly take the pen to create poetry (qtd. in Qian 40). In addition, Zhang Jiuzheng (1617–1684) suggests that masters in history all accomplish their literary achievements through acquired cultivation and personal efforts but that Ming Gong is bestowed with inborn and unique genius (Ibid.). By quoting lines from the poems created by these poets, Qian supports his idea that "talent" performs a decisive and irreplaceable function in transforming art and emotion into great masterpieces of poetry. In fact, Qian's discussion of "talent" here reminds us of Plato's idea of inspiration and Yan Yu's idea of "spontaneous enlightenment." All are beyond human beings' grasp and control, all are derived from supernatural or divine origins, and all are regarded as a supreme gift and the priority of selected poets.

Yet, although Qian Zhongshu acknowledges the existence of "genius" or "bestowed talent," he still considers the cultivation of the classic and rules of "art" indispensable. At the end of the chapter, Qian shifts the tone and suggests that "although this is the case (with the gifted genius), and there are indeed people who learn but are not capable of literary achievement, people who are gifted and talented must cultivate themselves and learn" (Qian 40). Qian asserts that "the excellence of great masters" cannot be independent of "rules" (Ibid.). Such a sense of "rules" must be cultivated by exploring and learning about the classic and tradition (Ibid.).

Like his predecessors, Qian Zhongshu notices the paradoxical relationship between the counterparts in literary creation. Aside from the discussion about emotion, art, and talent, in another chapter, "Imitating Nature and Improving Nature," of the same book, *Tan Yi Lu,* Qian talks about another element that is related to poetry creation. From the title of the chapter, we can easily see the premise that nature also participates in the process of producing poetry. In this chapter, Qian addresses the question of how to balance nature and literature in literary creation. *Nature*, as Qian defines at the beginning of the chapter, refers to that of the supreme and supernatural power. It is similar to Liu Xie's idea that literature is born with Heaven and Earth. Nature, like Heaven, has the prestige and perfection that enables it to be respected and imitated. Qian suggests that there are three ways for people to deal with nature: imitate nature, improve nature, or connect with nature (Ibid. 60). Qian reviews two streams of insights that strive to address the relationship between nature and literature and that enlighten us about the problem of how to adopt nature into literature. Some, as Qian introduces, regard nature's beauty as ready and perfect to be imitated in literary works. Only a careful selection of beauties ("selective imitation") within the natural world should be conducted beforehand (Ibid.). Qian takes Han Yu, who is considered one of the most renowned masters of literature in Chinese literary history, as an example. A line in his poem "To Answer Meng Jiao" reads *"wen zi qu tian qiao,"* meaning that words selectively observe the perfection of Heaven (Ibid.). Such an idea, as Qian suggests, corresponds exactly with the belief and appeal in imitating nature. Qian highly approves of Han Yu's use of the word *qu* here because it not only reveals how poets observe and imitate the beauty and perfection of nature, but it also indicates poets' initiative to choose between beauty and nature (Ibid.). Poets are not merely submissive to nature; they have their own wills and are capable of selecting and judging. This idea is not confined to Chinese literary history. Qian even quotes Shakespeare to illustrate the exemplar function of nature. As Qian quotes, Shakespeare, in his play *Hamlet*, says "to hold, as't were, the mirror up to nature" (qtd. in Qian 60).

Another stream of thought concerning the relationship between nature and literature claims that nature should be revised and improved. Scholars who endorse such ideas suppose that nature can only provide poets with raw and primitive materials (Qian 61): It is only when nature is processed and refined by the human mind that it can be as excellent as art, which is ideally created and polished by human intelligence (Ibid.). Qian gives erudite references to explain this idea. The scope of quotations is so wide that it ranges from Dio Chrysostom to Dante (Ibid. 60–61). None of these scholars, as Qian summarizes, yields individual creativity to a supernatural and divine power; rather, they emphasize the importance of individual intelligence and talent in refining and improving nature.

In fact, like most of his predecessors who hold impartial attitudes toward the two contrasting counterparts, Qian suggests a paradoxical relationship between nature and the human mind: They contrast with as well as complement each other. The relationship between nature and human intelligence is not a matter of superiority or inferiority but is rather a matter of inter-dependence and interaction. Human intelligence originates in nature and, in turn, nurtures the beauty of nature. Just as Qian's quotation of Shakespeare's lines suggests, "This is an art/Which does mend nature, change it rather, but/That art itself is Nature" (qtd. in Qian 61). It is as if, as Qian illuminates, nature is revising and perfecting itself by the hand of human beings, whose intelligence is attributed to nature. Such a paradoxical relationship, as Qian summarizes, reflects how the operation of the "supernatural and mysterious" power of nature and the performance of the "delicate and great mind" of human beings integrate with each other (Qian 62). The two are inseparable (Ibid.).

Nature and literature therefore enjoy a harmonious balance. Human minds imitate nature while at the same time individual intelligence refines nature. Nature is not an absolutely overwhelming entity that dictates individual creativity, nor is human intelligence polished enough to be detached from nature. Such a paradoxical relationship between nature and human thinking has been discussed and supported by great minds throughout Chinese history.

Yet, in Qian's contemporary time, another two prominent figures in Western literary history, Ernest Fenollosa (1853–1908) and Ezra Pound (1885–1972), propose a claim that derails the consistent and impartial discussion of nature in both Chinese and Western literary history. Fenollosa and Pound take a biased perspective and misunderstand Chinese written characters and poetry. Unlike Qian, who suggests a reciprocal and inter-dependent balance between nature and literature, they only emphasize one side of the problem. As Fenollosa and Pound assume, Chinese written characters only mechanically and superficially imitate nature without any processing of the abstract and metaphysical thinking of the human mind. Some even take such an idea as evidence to enhance a prejudice that Chinese language and literature are in stark contrast to Western culture. To them, Chinese thought and literature do not contain any of the metaphysical thinking that features in the Western thinking style.

To Fenollosa and Pound, Chinese people in ancient times yield themselves completely to the prestige and perfection of nature. They seem to worship the power of nature to such an extent that the desire to imitate nature is too overwhelming to resist. Even their language, which is the medium of communication between human minds, becomes a product of nature. Although it resonates with Aristotle's statement that tragedy begins because of humans' desire to imitate, the Chinese language, as some scholars suppose, is inferior due to the lack of abstract thinking. Fenollosa, in the book *The Chinese Written Character as a Medium of Poetry,* suggests that "examination shows that a

large number of the primitive Chinese characters, even the so-called radicals, are shorthand pictures of actions or processes" (Fenollosa and Pund 46). It
60 seems to Fenollosa that Chinese people can only perform simple imitation, as it requires none of the abstract thinking that enables Western people to relate phonetics to meanings. The imitation is seeable and can be corresponded with its material counterpart in nature. It is simpler than establishing an untouchable relationship between sounds and ideas, which belong to two different systems. To Fenollosa and Pound, Chinese thought and literature therefore take nature as the original and depend on it, but this does not work the other way around or in both ways, as Qian and his predecessors suggest.

Zhang Longxi, in his article "The 'Tao' and the 'Logos': Notes on Derrida's Critique of Logocentrism" rebuts Fenollosa's idea. Zhang suggests that to view Chinese written characters in ideograms and to emphasize the pictorial value of them can be misleading and imposes misinterpretation and discrimination on Chinese thought and literature. Zhang takes Ezra Pound's translation of *Confucian Analects* as an example. The Chinese written character "習," as Zhang quotes, has been translated as "white feature" in Pound's translation of *Confucian Analects*. This unreasonably twists the original meaning of the character, which is "to practice" (Zhang Longxi, "The 'Tao' and the 'Logos'" 389). Zhang explains how this self-fancied interpretation ridiculously transforms the original meaning of the analects:

> This character appears in the first sentence of the *Confucian Analects*, which could be translated as: "The Master says: to learn and to practice from time to time — is this not a joy?" In his fervent anatomy of Chinese script, however, Pound seized upon the feather image and rendered the line as: "Study with the seasons winging past, is not this pleasant?" (Ibid.).

The Chinese character "習" is viewed as a picture in Pound's translation. Pound separates the character into two parts: the upper part, "羽," meaning "feather" and the lower part, "白," meaning "white." To Pound, such an approach is innovating and unique, introducing a stream of freshness to the tradition of the Western world. Pound's fascination with the natural interpretation of Chinese characters and poetry, however, indicates a sense of discrimination against Chinese culture and literature, which, as some Western scholars presume, belong to the "other." To these scholars, the Chinese characters do not have any consistent thoughts behind them. They merely extend before readers as parts of pictures that mechanically imitate and mirror the natural objects. The different parts of which the characters are composed do not have a logical inter-relationship between them but are simply juxtaposed with each other.

In fact, such a "nature" interpretation of Chinese characters and poetry is merely a self-fancied invention that caters to Western scholars' expectation to find something new. It is not a reliable or reasonable way to understand Chinese literature and culture. Zhang quotes T. S. Eliot's words to support his refutation against Pound's idea. Eliot suggests that Pound's works "will be called (and justly) a 'magnificent specimen of XXth-century poetry rather than a 'translation'" (qtd. in Zhang Longxi, "The 'Tao' and the 'Logos'" 390). Eliot even sarcastically comments that "Pound is the inventor of Chinese poetry for our time" (Ibid.). Indeed, Fenollosa and Pound are mistaken in claiming that Chinese characters and poetry only imitate nature, and to downgrade Chinese culture and literature because of the assumption that it lacks logical and metaphysical thinking is also discriminating and refutable. Such an imprudent assertion has already been rebutted by our review here concerning the paradoxical relationship between the classic and creativity and also between nature and literature. From as early as the time of *The Book of Poetry* to modern times, Chinese ancient and contemporary literary critics and masterminds have always noticed and acknowledged the paradoxical relationship between the counterparts in the process of literary creation. These discussions and arguments certainly require metaphysical and logical thinking and reasoning, and they are no less comprehensive or adequate when compared with those of Western critics and scholars. The correspondence and affinities between Chinese and Western scholars, in fact, become the most convincing evidence for arguing against the attempt to dichotomize or to discriminate between cultures.

Chapter Three

The Classic and Canon as "Means of Discrimination"

It is difficult to determine whether we are fortunate to have the classic. On one hand, gratitude should always be properly conveyed, as generations have been enlightened by those great minds and profound thoughts preserved in great works. Figures of prominence are readily presented to us. Their insight and intelligence nurture our minds and tastes, and their achievements enable us to make further progress. Yet, grateful as we are, to conform to the classic and tradition also seems to impede the efforts of those who strive to regenerate and revitalize the classic. The power and influence of the classic and tradition can be so almighty and overwhelming that they can overshadow every single thing that is labeled as individual or creative. Those who dare to claim that they are new and individual are unlikely to gain approval or even to survive. It is even less possible for the avant-gardes to muster up the courage to interrogate the authority of the classic and tradition or to improve and renew the classic and tradition.

To re-examine the role of the classic in the history of literature development and its relationship with individual creativity is of significance for the time being. Criticism and negative views about the classic are constantly voiced.. Some disapprove of the concept of the classic because to rigidly prioritize the classic is to advocate a sense of elite conceit and to exacerbate the stubborn prejudice against popularization. Emerging theories such as postmodernism, poststructuralism, and especially postcolonialism all hold negative attitudes toward authorization and canonization. Such situations naturally evoke the question of why the classic is blamed for being elite and discriminating. In addressing this question, we cannot avoid tracing back to the origin and definition of the classic and reviewing prejudices that have resulted in the provincial and parochial image of the classic.

Saving the classic from being reduced to tools that propagate cultural bias is more urgent in this age of world literature. Different cultures have their own list of canons. The classic from so-called "centered" cultures may have the privilege to acquire a cosmopolitan reputation and readership. Literature from less popular or familiar cultures may be neglected or even rejected. Yet is this fair and valid? The ascendance and success of the concept of world literature today encourages exchange and communication between different cultures and literatures. To establish a closed circle of the classic from "centered cultures" only will certainly impede positive circulation and communication worldwide. To ignore the excellence of literatures from less familiar cultures and to fence them off from the closed circle of the classic not only makes the classic miss the chance to renew and improve so as to fit in with different contexts and times but also deprives readers from different places and times of exposure to more excellence produced by human minds. Therefore, opening up the list of the classic is of lateral benefit.

3.1 Confined Definition: The Classic and Ancient Greek and Latin Literature

Then how has the classic become a symbol of closed elitism? T. S. Eliot begins his widely renowned poem *The Waste Land* with the sentence "April is the cruelest month," expressing a kind of solitude and melancholy that is prompted by the situation where the old die with the new unborn. The classic, if confined to periods or cultures that are too limited, may suffer from similar situations, where the old traditions are gone with the golden old days while the new and contemporary are denied access and acknowledgement from the

64 established circle of the classic. For this reason, the classic may be blamed for being parochial and provincial. Definitions of the word *classic* also contribute to such prejudice. In the *Oxford English Dictionary,* for example, the word *classic* as a noun has been defined as follows:

a. An ancient Greek or Latin writer or literary work, of the first rank and of acknowledged excellence; any one of a body of ancient Greek or Latin writers or texts traditionally considered as the model for all literary endeavors. In later use usu. in pl. with the canon of ancient Greek and Latin literature.

b. A student of Greek and Latin literature, a classical scholar. Now rare.[1]

It may be unjust to judge whether the inclusion of these entries is improper, as the definitions have been determined by the word's etymology and its customary uses from early history. Such specific definitions of *classic* restricted to Greek and Latin cultures and things related to them, however, can inevitably lead to the uneasy feeling that the sacred sanctuary of the classic has already been taken and closed. The new and contemporary are denied the possibility to enter the sanctuary, let alone to replace and rebuild it. Living generations have no choice but to worship the already established sanctuary with eternal humbleness from outside or to rigidly adhere and conform to Greek and Latin tradition, which is defined as the "model of all literary endeavors." If this definition is upheld as a rule that needs to be inflexibly observed, individual creativity or originality that deviates from Greek and Latin traditions must be eliminated from the classic. Ernest Hemingway in his Nobel speech instructed writers to "try for something that has never been done or that others have tried to do and failed" (Hemingway), but he immediately changes his tone and adds that "then, sometimes, with great luck, he will succeed" (Ibid.). Greek and Latin cultures are regarded as the origins of Western culture. Their prestige and authority are never to be denied or disregarded. Overlooking them in literary creation is not an easy task or a wise attempt. Everything new in literary creation should be related to Greek and

---

[1] "classic, adj. and n." *OED Online* Oxford University Press, December 2014. Web. 30 January 2015.

Latin cultures and literatures. Such conformity is monotonous and frustrating. It is difficult to escape the haunting influence of Greek and Latin culture authorized by the definition and recognized by the majority and by history. No wonder Hemingway sarcastically suggests that originality needs "great luck" to achieve acknowledgment and recognition. In this sense, the classic, if given definitions that are too restricted, frustrate individual creativity by refusing to approve any new achievements or attempts.

Such definitions not only impede the development of individual creativity, but they also indicate cultural discrimination. To attach importance and honor to Greek and Latin cultures is reasonable, but to make them exclusive and superior is questionable. This is particularly refutable when it comes to this age of world literature, when diversity is appreciated and open-mindedness is valued. Segregating classics and cultures and impeding their circulation and exchange of ideas and perspectives will render the ghettoized classics and cultures stagnant without further development or progress.

3.2　T. S. Eliot: Tradition and Depersonalization

T. S. Eliot can be regarded as a conservative figure. His eagerness to stress the significance of the classic can be interpreted as a gesture to protect the conceit of the elite. Eliot generously gives his praise to Virgil in "What Is a Classic" and attaches high importance to Roman culture, both of which are symbolic of Eliot's erudition and cultivation. Compared to his attitudes toward the classic and tradition, Eliot's opinion about individual creativity is less serious. He downplays the role and function of individual creativity and personal feelings in the process of literary creation. To Eliot, individual creativeness does not participate in literary creation but rather only serves as a catalyst, like that in chemical reactions. Individuality and personal feelings, as Eliot suggests, are only to stimulate and inspire.

In fact, what Eliot advocates in poetry creation is a kind of "depersonalization." In another famous article written by T. S Eliot, "Tradition and the Individual Talent," Eliot argues that what matters to a poet is "the consciousness of the past," which he or she "should continue to develop ...

66 throughout his career" (Eliot, *The Sacred Wood* 30). Individual creativity and personal feelings, conversely, should be covered, compromised, and even eliminated. Eliot suggests that "what happens is a continual surrender of himself as he is at the moment to something which is more valuable" (Ibid.). "The progress of an artist," as Eliot asserts, "is a continual self-sacrifice, a continual extinction of personality" (Ibid.). Eliot, again, refers to the analogy of the chemical reaction to illustrate the depersonalization process:

> There remains to define this process of depersonalization and its relation to the sense of tradition. It is in this depersonalization that art may be said to approach the condition of science. I shall, therefore, invite you to consider, as a suggestive analogy, the action which takes place when a bit of finely filiated platinum is introduced into a chamber containing oxygen and sulphur dioxide. (Ibid.)

Individual talent, in this sense, is pathetically and unfairly sacrificed. Not only does Eliot emphasize the inferiority of individual talent to tradition and the classic in the process of creating literature, but he also indicates that the classic and tradition serve as measures that select and even discriminate between individual talent. When introducing the indispensable conditions under which the classic works are produced, Eliot touches on the idea of "maturity." Maturity, as Eliot explains, refers to maturity in three aspects: maturity in language, maturity in literature, and maturity in mind. "Maturity" also refers to "the importance of language to that civilization and society" and the "comprehensiveness of an individual mind" (Eliot, "What Is a Classic" 10). Horizontally, maturity represents the highest level of excellence achieved by the classic works when compared with contemporary literatures. Vertically, maturity is attributed to the constant progresses of the classic throughout time and history. To recognize what is maturity and to appreciate it requires much more than a mere literal understanding of the classic works. Not only should a mature mind be knowledgeable about literary facts and history and be familiar with their meanings and significance, but a mature mind is also expected to be equipped with better aesthetic values and tastes. Those who are not fortunate enough to be bestowed with the capability to apprehend and appreciate the "maturity" of the classic, to Eliot, are fenced off from the elite and closed circle of the classic. Eliot suggests that "to make the meaning of maturity really apprehensible — indeed, even to make it acceptable — to the immature, is perhaps impossible" (Ibid.). Few except those great minds who have already gained wide approval dare to boast that they have acquired the quality to contribute to "maturity." Less qualified individuals are refused access to this sacred and elite domain of the classic.

The inferiority of individuals' creativeness in literary creation is also reflected through their dependence on the classic and tradition. The destiny of creativity is determined and evaluated by the classic and tradition. When Eliot describes how individual talent functions in literature, he refers to three different periods in which creativity is viewed differently. In ages that precede the classic age, individuality, which is indeed "eccentricity," can be accepted and acknowledged due to the lack of the sense of "correctness" (Ibid. 14); in the age that follows the classic age, the "eccentricity" is taken as a symbol of hope in contrast to the barrenness that resulted from the exhaustive exploration of the classic age (Ibid.). In the classic age, individual style becomes "subtle" and internalized, "refined" by the "common style" and is concealed behind the "common style" (Ibid.). As Eliot implies, the positive impression about individual talent in ages before and after the classic age is wrongly formed. It does not deserve recognition. In the classic age, individual talent is covered and shadowed by the highlight of the classic. It is invisible and subjective to the classic and tradition; it has to compromise and yield to the sense of "correctness" and "refinement."

Even worse is that individual talent has no way to overcome such oppression by the classic and tradition. Literary works resemble children in the way that individual creativity is genetically and inevitably impacted by the classic and tradition, just like children inherit "family characteristics" and "ancestral traits" from their paternal and maternal generations (Ibid.). Although they are unconscious of these internally bestowed features and genes, children's behaviors and dispositions are surely attributed to the inheritance. Individual creativity may "revolt" in adolescence and rejoice at their courageous attempts to renounce the destined inheritance (Ibid.). Yet "in retrospect," as Eliot proceeds, when time has allowed the individual enough distance to review history as an outsider, he or she will find that "he [or she] is also the continuer of their traditions, that he [or she] preserves essential family characteristics, and that his [or her] difference in behavior is a difference in the circumstances of another age" (Ibid.).

It is frustrating to be informed that however hard one impoverishes his or her talent and struggles for something new, he or she can hardly escape the impact of the classic and tradition that has been "manipulating" him or her. What they rejoice at are just illusions cast on a "superficial appearance," beneath which is the irremovable "genetic constituents." Overshadowed by their fathers' generations, whose excellence can be exhaustive and whose influence is irresistible, individuals who resolve to surpass their precedents will be frustrated. Eliot compassionately comments that their "hope for the future is founded upon the attempt to renounce the past" (Ibid. 15).

The classic serves as measures that determine, evaluate, and even discriminate between individual talent. The overwhelming prestige and influence of the classic is never to be questioned. At the same time, however, Eliot does not hold the belief that the classic should be confined to a specific time or culture. This idea is revealed through our previous discussion about the three features of the "inclusiveness" of the classic. Instead of being restricted to one perfect period or focused on a single figure, the characteristics of the classic are reflected chronically in different periods within the same culture, or geographically in different contemporary cultures. In addition, the classic should not refuse interdisciplinary approaches. The virtue of diversity is essential for a genuine piece of the classic. It enables scholars with different research interests and specializations to find what deserves to be studied. Scholars' studies, however, can only exhaust certain aspects but never the whole piece because interdisciplinary approaches have provided inexhaustible perspectives for study, and this is exactly the charm of diversity for a genuine piece of the classic. Culturally, the classic is also far-reaching. Exchanges of the classic works between different cultures and exposure to diverse excellence received from different classic works from different cultures benefit both the original and target cultures.

3.3 Woolf: The Male-Dominated Classic and Discrimination Against Female Talent ─────

Virginia Woolf (1882–1941) can be regarded as a pioneer who enlightens and initiates efforts to awaken the awareness of feminism. Unlike Eliot, who generally comments on the selective and eliminating feature of the classic when it relates to individual talent, Woolf adopts a more specific perspective. In her most representative work, *A Room of One's Own*, Woolf initiates firm protests against the male-dominated classic system. As Woolf suggests, it denies the value of female creativity and refuses to accept and acknowledge it as part of the classic. She also utters an earnest appeal for female writers to change this disadvantaged situation. In Eliot's "What Is a Classic," it is the utmost excellence of the classic that intimidates and threatens the development of individual creativity. In Woolf's opinion, however, it is the defect of the classic, namely, the rude exclusion of female writers' contribution, that becomes the obstacle hindering the progress of female creativity. Unlike Eliot, who supports his idea by reminding us of the "retrospect," Woolf encourages us to hold "foresights" that foresee an ideal system of the classic where female creativity functions as an indispensable part.

The first unreasonable aspect of the classic in her contemporary time, as Woolf argues, is the irrational prejudice and cruel inferiority that are imposed upon female creativity. The male-dominated literary society deliberately and obstinately leaves the field of female writing barren and uncultivated. Conventional beliefs that females are not sufficiently qualified to produce works that count as the classic results in a severe oppression of female talent and creativity. Male writers holding such beliefs are to blame. Although she conveys them through a stream of unconsciousness and a story-telling pattern, Woolf does not confuse her clear logic and accurateness in sharply pointing out the defects of the classic system of her time, nor does she weaken her voice in interrogating the inappropriateness of the ideas of those male writers who unjustifiably defend male superiority and priority. Ellen Bayuk Rosenman, in the book *A Room of One's Own: Women Writers and the Politics of Creativity*, suggests,

> Masterpieces are not created in isolation, without context or history. Instead, Woolf claims, they are the culmination of a tradition, and they can only flower in a material environment that supports — or at least does not impede — the artist. Women, living in a male world, lack the necessary autonomy to create freely. (Rosenman 29)

Woolf depicts those male figures of rude conceit sarcastically: "I had been drawing a face, a figure. It was the face and the figure of Professor von X engaged in writing his monumental work entitled *The Mental, Moral, and Physical Inferiority of the Female Sex*" (Woolf 24). The title of the fictionalized book is offensive. Although this is an illusory mental image, it genuinely reflects the cruel reality where female writers suffer. To Woolf, the male writer has always been "protesting against the equality of the other sex by asserting his own superiority" (Ibid. 76). Male writers' conceit has been supported by the unfairly established priority of male writers who have taken the biased advantage for granted for a long time. Female writers, when approaching this defective system of the classic, will find nothing related to their own creativity and perspectives:

> Do what she will a woman cannot find in them that fountain of perpetual life which the critics assure her is there. It is not only that they celebrate male virtues, enforce male values and describe the world of men: it is that the emotion with which these books are permeated is to a woman incomprehensible. (Ibid. 77)

To exclude and fence off female creativity and perspectives renders the circle of the classic closed and incomplete. The scope of the classic will become more stagnant and unaccomplished if they insist on the biased inclusion of only males' works. Not only can female creativity provide different perspectives and expand the vision and scope of the classic, but female writers with their advantages and expertise can also compensate for what is lacking in male writings. As Woolf suggests, "thus all their (male) writers' qualities seem to a woman, if one may generalize, crude and immature. They lack suggestive power. And when a book lacks suggestive power, however hard it hits the surface of the mind it cannot penetrate within" (Ibid.).

The difference between those biased male writers and real masters who impartially embrace alterity and diversity can be obvious. Woolf takes one of the male critics, Mr. B, whom she fabricates, or rather, whom she uses to mirror someone in real life, as a representative of the male writers who hold fierce prejudice against female writers. His counterpart is Coleridge, whose work, to Woolf, is indeed inexhaustible, complete, and "perpetual":

> Very able they (male writers) were, acute and full of learning; but the trouble was that his feelings no longer communicated; his mind seemed separated into different chambers; not a sound carried from one to the other. Thus, when one takes a sentence of Mr. B into the mind it falls plump to the ground — dead; but when one takes a sentence of Coleridge into the mind, it explodes and gives birth to all kinds of other ideas, and that is the only sort of writing of which one can say that it has the secret of perpetual life. (Ibid.)

Resonating with Eliot, Woolf also values the "inclusiveness" of the classic. If female talent and creativity are included, the classic will be more universal, enjoying enduring popularity and interest. Woolf asserts that "doubtless Elizabethan literature would have been very different from what it is if the women's movement had begun in the sixteenth century and not in the nineteenth" (Ibid. 76).

Male writers' despising and denial of females' talent and creativity is rightly condemned. Their unjustified attempts to take the classic creation as the priority of male writers are no less severe than the efforts that tend to use the classic to discriminate or eliminate individual talents that are less fortunate to be bestowed with quality to appreciate and create the classic. The prejudice of those male writers seems to be less grounded, as they judge by genders, which is hardly a measure by which to evaluate one's talent and creativity.

An unpleasant yet inevitable result of such an unhealthy context for female writers is that female writers are not directed or modified by the tradition and the classic of their own. They need to break through the barriers and start from scratch. The talent and creativity of female writers have long been neglected. They do not have the opportunity or time to establish an archive that shades later generations. They have no predecessors to turn to when they are confused about their own creations. They do not have a carefully designed style that caters to their own needs. They do not have customized methods of expression with which they are familiar and can freely adopt in their creations. They have to take the risk of being criticized or rejected when they muster up the courage to try something new. They do not have the chance to show in an ideal way their sensibility, which is female writers' symbolic advantage. Woolf expresses with sincere pity that such a deficiency and lack of female contribution is a great loss for the classic:

> Indeed, since freedom and fullness of expression are of the essence of the art, such a lack of tradition, such a scarcity and inadequacy of tools, must have torn enormously upon the writings of women. Moreover, a book is not made of sentences laid end to end, but of sentence built, if an image helps, into arcades or domes. And this shape too has been made by men out of their own needs for their own uses. (Ibid. 58)

The barrenness in the field of female writings not only handicaps female talent and creativity but also forces females to compromise with regard to the existing rules of writing, which are not suitable for their delicate form of expression. They have to sacrifice their intentions and goals. To survive the disadvantaged environment, women writers, against their will, may even shelter under less mature fields of writing. As Woolf suggests, most female writers choose novels as their writing debut. This is not an unexpected coincidence. The reason for females' fairly active participation in novel writing is that the form of novel writing has a shorter history than traditional forms such as poems or verses: The longer the history, the more difficult it is to be accepted as part of it. Female writers, owing to this reason, mostly choose the "pliable" form of the novel, expecting a less hampered entry into literature (Ibid.). It is reasonable for Woolf to propose the idea that we should have "foresight" rather than "retrospect" when it comes to the classic. If female writers look back, they have again endured the miserable history of being discriminated against and isolated. They have to muster up courage and look forward to a different future, although they need to expend much effort, the amount of which is unexpected, for such a future.

Regardless of their diverging opinions concerning whether to have "retrospect" or "foresight" for the classic, Woolf's proposal of forming an unconscious unity between the two genders resonates with Eliot, who promotes "an unconscious balance" between the classic and individual creativity. "Unconscious" is in the sense that female writers should be disarmed with hostility toward males. They should strive to express and convey their true and independent insights rather than waste their words and utter mere protests against males. This idea, to some extent, corresponds with Eliot's words that a conscious refusal of the classic is neither feasible nor beneficial for individual creativity.

The sense of unity means that female writers not only free themselves from the negative feelings against males but also, unlike their counterparts, male writers who prioritize and focus only on their own perspectives, acquire the capability to adopt angles that can reflect both females' and males' ways of thinking during their process of writing. Rather than regarding the two genders as dichotomies or enemies, Woolf suggests a harmonious integration of the two genders in literary creation, and what is achieved at last is a kind of "unity of mind." Such an idea, again, reminds us of Eliot's "unconscious balance":

> What does one mean by "the unity of mind"? I pondered, for clearly the mind has so great a power of concentrating at any point at any moment that it seems to have no single state of being. It can separate itself from the people in the street, for example, and think of itself as apart from them, at an upper window looking down on them. (Ibid. 73)

Portraying a boy and a girl entering the same taxi, Woolf stands high and looks out of the window, as an outsider with a comprehensive and detached overview. By designing such a plot, Woolf means to convey two meanings. Females and males are neither enemies who can never coexist, nor are they passersby who can never meet or know each other. Once joined together, they can constitute a harmonious and satisfying group. Instead of involving themselves in hatred and lingering as part of the dichotomy between genders, female writers can step aside, relieve themselves of their personal experiences of misery, and simply enjoy such an enchanted moment of harmony as spectators. Supported by Coleridge's ideas about an "androgynous" mind that "transmits emotion without impediments" and that is "naturally creative, incandescent, and undivided" (Ibid. 74), Woolf appeals to female writers to cultivate a kind of conscious ignorance of distinctions between females and males, pursuing the correspondence of minds "with other people spontaneously" (Ibid. 73).

If female writers are too involved in their long-accumulated hatred toward males or too indulged in their revolt against the male-dominated classic, their writings cannot have genuine or ingenious insights. If female writers are so obsessed with intolerable differences between the genders and so conscious of the miserable suppression created by males, their literary productions will be reduced to monotonous and shallow complaints and protests, which will waste their talent to search for more profound truths and their time to conduct more rewarding exploration. Woolf notices such negative side effects of feminism. She warns that it would be quite a pity if their "natural advantages of a higher order" and "wide, eager and free" sensibility were replaced by such negative dispositions (Ibid. 70). To be indulged in these negative feelings is to trap female writers themselves into a worse situation, where they are manipulated by males' ideas and feelings. Woolf presents with earnest compassion the example of Charlotte Brontë, whose enviable gifts are overshadowed by her too deliberate attempts to regain what she has been deprived of (Ibid. 58).

In contrast to Brontë, Woolf presents with rejoiced surprise the example of Mary Carmichael as an ideal female writer who, although less talented, manages to disregard labels of sex and gender and simply expresses fluently what she needs to convey as a writer instead of as a female writer. Woolf remains fierce and harsh in tone all through A Room of One's Own, with few exceptions where her female sensitivity inevitably overflows. One of these exceptions is where she attaches sincere approval and appreciation to Mary Carmichael, modeling her into one who extinguishes the firing hatred that is growing in her contemporary female writers:

> She had certain advantages which women of far greater gift lacked even half a
> century ago. Men were no longer to her "the opposing faction"; she need not waste
> her time railing against them; she need not climb onto the roof or ruin her peace of
> mind longing for travel, experience and a knowledge of the world and character that
> were denied her. Fear and hatred were almost gone, or traces of them showed only
> in a slight exaggeration of the joy of freedom, a tendency to the caustic and satirical,
> rather than to the romantic, in her treatment of the other sex. (Ibid. 70)

Aside from "unity," another element that nourishes female writing is the
efforts made by the predecessors of female writers. Although Woolf holds
quite critical attitudes toward the classic that is produced and protected by
males, she highly praises the classic and tradition that have been diligently and
fearlessly established by women writers under the unfriendly contexts. Woolf
even acknowledges the significance of these classic works as solid ground for
new attempts in female writing. Like Eliot, Woolf regards such a foundation as
necessary preparation for female writing to achieve a kind of "maturity." Eliot
explains in "What Is a Classic" that "an individual author, notably Shakespeare
and Virgil, can do much to develop his language, but he cannot bring that
language to maturity unless the work of his predecessors has prepared it for his
final touch" (Eliot, "What Is a Classic" 11). Any new heights reached or new
moves conducted in language or literary works should always be attributed to
the classic, to "the history behind it," which consists of "an ordered though
unconscious progress of a language to realize its own potentialities within its
own limitations" (Ibid.).

Woolf thinks alike. She reminds us that we should not forget the
miserable yet formidable, rewarding as well as enlightening endeavors made
by predecessors of female writers. Woolf takes Aphra Benn and Jane Austen
as representatives of the predecessors. Thanks to Benn's courageous debut
of female writing in those horrible ages where female writers earned nothing
but abuse and contempt, female writers of later times will not be intimated on
their way to breaking down the barriers (Woolf 48).

Mary Carmichael, for example, as Woolf describes in *A Room of One's*

Own, bravely and innovatively tried to touch on the relationships between females themselves. The short sentence containing only three simple words, "Chloe liked Olivia," to Woolf, is already a huge step forward in female writing (Ibid. 63). Female writers begin to focus on themselves without involving or relating to males. They are independent and become focused on females themselves. As Woolf suggests, what Carmichael does is "to catch those unrecorded gestures, those unsaid or half-said words" that were previously missing due to the sad fact that female writers have been "so terribly accustomed to suppression and concealment" (Ibid. 64). "[Feeling] the light fall on it," as Woolf excitedly comments, Carmichael "reaches for this organism that has been under the shadow of the rock these million years" (Ibid.).

"Light," as Woolf here indicates, is the inspiring power that is kindled by predecessors for late comers, and it is the light that motivates and directs Carmichael's bold attempts and ways ahead. Carmichael is prepared rather than discouraged when encountering similar evils. Strengthening and hardening herself, Carmichael manages to "go without kindness and condescension but in the spirit of fellowship in those small, scented rooms" (Ibid. 67).

Austen, conversely, brings female writings to prosperity or comparative maturity, based upon which later generations, including Carmichael and other female writers, can progress with promising and surprising breakthroughs. Female writers of later generations can attribute their efforts to these predecessors, but with due respect, they can also improve on what their predecessors achieved. Austen is exampled as a model whose conventionally approved ways designed for female writing have been refined and improved by Carmichael, who strikes readers with untraditional elements such as "broken sequence" and unnatural "order" (Ibid. 69). It is not that female writers of later generations overlook what has been greatly achieved by their predecessors, but it is only with such critical attitudes that the literary traditions of female writing can witness constant improvements. To be "lazy minded" will disable female writers, precluding them from inheriting and improving the "serious, profound and humane" created by their predecessors (Ibid.).

With all female writers' preparations, Carmichael is ready to explore deeper territory on her way to developing female writing. Although Woolf warns that there is intimidating unpredictability lying before her, as Carmichael "will light a torch in that vast chamber where nobody has yet been" (Ibid. 63), Woolf still gives generous encouragement to Carmichael, talking about "holding your torch firm in your hand" (Ibid. 68). Woolf would be most disappointed if the "light" extinguished; however, with the unity of genders and unity of mind and with the foundation laid by predecessors of female writers and critical attitudes, Carmichael and her contemporaries, and later generations of female writers, are the most prepared to extend the history of female writing.

3.4 Harold Bloom: The Western Canon for Pure Aesthetic Value and "Achieved Individuality" ——

The concept of the classic may be discriminating when it excludes readers that are not considered elites. Sometimes it only selects contributors by gender. It can also become judgmental when it rejects new approaches of studies. Harold Bloom (1930–), for example, in his famous and controversial book *The Western Canon,* makes an urgent appeal to scholars, urging them to enclose literature studies within the realm of aesthetics. To Bloom, any attempts to expand the classic and literary studies to anything beyond aesthetics are rightly condemned. Any purpose other than pursuing beauty and purity is pathetic and invalid. To politicize literature studies and to expand literature studies to cultural studies are both regarded as indecent approaches. The classic is therefore for individuals who are capable of acknowledging the aesthetic value of it.

By deliberately using the word *canon* instead of *classic* in the title of the book, Bloom enhances the discriminating feature of the classic. Unlike entries for *classic* and *tradition,* which consist of definitions that focus on conveying a sense of abstract excellence and consistency and feature no tracing back to concrete and material objects, explanations for *canon* attribute the word to its etymology as a practical tool of measurement. Some scholars suggest that the word originates as "a measuring rod," which appears in Sumerian, Babylonian, and Semitic concepts (Carravetta 264). By attaching the word to historical existence, the definition solidifies its accuracy as an irrefutable concept.

Canon is indeed to be used to measure and select, and its etymology makes people suppose that *canon* denotes a more specific concept and is thus more effective and aggressive than *the classic* and *tradition* when it evaluates individual creativity. Conforming to *canon* seems to be a more obligatory act: *Canon* enforces its law more powerfully; the authority and enforcement of it are never to be questioned. The entries in the *Oxford English Dictionary* all reflect and enhance such features. Let us review the first five definitions given in the dictionary here:

> A rule, law, or decree of the Church; esp. a rule laid down by an ecclesiastical Council;
>
> Canon law n. (formerly law canon: cf. French droit canon): ecclesiastical law, as laid down in decrees of the pope and statutes of councils;
>
> A law, rule, edict (other than ecclesiastical);
>
> A general rule, fundamental principle, aphorism, or axiom governing the systematic or scientific treatment of a subject; e.g. canons of descent or inheritance; A logical, grammatical, or metrical canon; canons of criticism, taste, art, etc.;
>
> A standard of judgement or authority; a test, criterion, means of discrimination.[1]

Law, decree, rule, principle, standard, and criterion all define the essence of the word *canon*. Its authority is indisputable and supreme. Law means that we should never disobey it. Decree means that we should never defy it. Principle means that we should never violate it. Standard and criterion means that we should never challenge it. Canons are like this. The first three entries all refer to law, either ecclesiastical or not, enhancing the authority of *canon*. When *canon* refers to literature or art instead of law, its prestige and power

---

[1] "Canon, n.1." *OED Online*. Oxford University Press, December 2014. Web. 30 January 2015.

are not weakened. It embodies a set of principles that are "fundamental" and "general." It encompasses all kinds of excellences of the classic, and it only requires submissive conformity. The last entry for *canon*, quoted above, gives a more direct, more offensive, yet more factual definition. *Canon* can be "a standard of judgment or authority" and, what is worse, a "means of discrimination." *Canon* means to evaluate and judge, however eccentric or judgmental the criterion may be. In fact, *canon* with such indubitable authority not only attracts blind submission, which is intimidated by the overwhelming power of it, but it also prompts fierce rebuttal and critical denunciation. If *canon* is falsely used as a "means of discrimination," it is no longer authoritative but is rather authoritarian.

To Bloom, however, to use the selective and eliminating nature of *canon* is an academic gesture and attitude that should be rightly advocated. In Bloom's view, *canon*, then, is reduced to a "means of discrimination." He reinforces such ideas by indicating that *canon* discriminates against individuals who are not qualified enough to appreciate the aesthetic value of *canon* and that they should be refused access to study canons:

> We need to teach more selectively, searching for the few who have the capacity to become highly individual readers and writers. The others, who are amenable to a politicized curriculum, can be abandoned to it. Pragmatically, aesthetic value can be recognized or experienced, but it cannot be conveyed to those who are incapable of grasping its sensations and perceptions. To quarrel on its behalf is always a blunder. (Bloom 17)

Bloom freely and firmly expresses his insistence to take *canon* as a "means of discrimination." People who are "incapable of grasping its sensations and perceptions" are not only unfortunate in the sense that they are not bestowed with genius and a born gift, but it is also hopeless to cultivate them after they are born because "aesthetic value can be recognized or experienced, but it cannot be conveyed" to them. What is more pathetic is that they are even deprived of the right to utter opposing voices and to change such an inferior situation because Bloom suggests that "to quarrel on its behalf is always a blunder."

As Bloom proceeds with his argument, *canon* not only needs to fence off disqualified individuals but must also remain elite, closed, and purified. This

80 belongs to an elite group only:

> Aesthetic value is by definition engendered by an interaction between artists, an influencing that is always an interpretation. The freedom to be an artist, or a critic, necessarily rises out of social conflict. But the source or origin of the freedom to perceive, while hardly irrelevant to aesthetic value, is not identical with it. There is always guilt in achieved individuality; it is a version of the guilt of being a survivor, and is not productive of aesthetic value. (Ibid. 24)

Bloom is too harsh in saying these words. He goes to an unpleasant extreme when guarding the sacredness of canons. *Canon* and *the classic* become the labels of elitists, showing their priority and superiority. To Bloom, aesthetic values are to be appreciated and communicated by "artists" only. The aesthetic value of canons should remain elite and only authorized to a limited number of qualified individuals who, as Bloom asserts, "feel themselves chosen by ancestral figures" (Ibid. 20). Not everyone is entitled to access and achieve such values. The common majority, as Bloom indicates, neither deserves access to the canon and the classic, nor can they contribute to the aesthetic values of the canon and the classic. To let everyone "perceive" canon and the classic is only a compassionate and pretentious gesture by the elitists.

With such offensive words, Bloom prompts fierce criticism and needs to be rebutted and revised. To confine canon and the classic to the realm of elites frustrates individual creativity, and to reduce canon and the classic to a simple measure to select and discriminate is unacceptable. In fact, Bloom's insistence on making *canon* superior and elite is not supported by solid proof but rather by a vague argument and provincial prejudice. His adherence to closing the circle of canon and the classic seems to stem more from his fear than from his faith. Individuals with talent who are cultivated with canon and the classic can not only develop their own minds and capability, but they can also contribute to the appreciation of canon and the classic. Once open to more talents, Bloom feels threatened that what he is specialized in is not his priority and that he may even be replaced and surpassed. To guard his authority as a specialist and to extend his influence and priority, Bloom indulges himself with these unreasonable prejudices. The results can be devastating. Potential talents will never be found. Promising individual creativity will be frustrated. Canon and the classic, similarly, will suffer from unproductive barrenness and hopeless stagnation.

When defending the sacredness of the concept of *canon*, Bloom not only discriminates against people who were not lucky enough to be born with the capability to appreciate the aesthetic value but also negates the attempts to enrich studies of canons with insights from newly emerged schools of criticism. In "An Elegy for the Canon," the first article in *The Western Canon*, Bloom expresses without reservation his strong disapproval of "cultural criticism":

> Cultural criticism is another dismal social science, but literary criticism, as an art, always was and always will be an elitist phenomenon. It was a mistake to believe that literary criticism could become a basis for democratic education or for societal improvement. When our English and other literature departments shrink to the dimensions of our current classics departments, ceding their grosser functions to the legions of Cultural Studies, we will perhaps be able to return to the study of the inescapable, to Shakespeare and his few peers, who after all, invented all of us. (Ibid. 17)

To Bloom, the claim of common people to perceive canons freely and the attempt of emerging schools of criticism to broaden the researching scope of canons are just an excuse for their impotence in achieving the capability to appreciate the aesthetic value of canons. Bloom declares with no hesitation that the closed circle of canon and the classic will not and must not be "forced open" (Ibid. 35).

Cultural criticism and cultural studies as emerging disciplines, however, have garnered unexpected popularity, and their ascendance has been witnessed recently. Intimidated by this, Bloom appeals urgently, emphasizes greatly, and reminds us earnestly of the sacredness of canon and the classic. To Bloom, canon should not be violated by defiant approaches or unqualified entry; it should remain stable and unaltered as a kind of authorized measurement.

To enlarge and expand the scope of canons is unbearable to Bloom. Cultural criticism, however, which tolerates and validates "random" schools of criticism to approach canons, has prospered to an extent that is intolerable to Bloom. To cushion the strike upon the aesthetic value of canons resulting from the overwhelming intrusion of such "limitless idealism" of "cultural criticism," Bloom advocates and legitimizes the parochialism of canon, arguing that canon "exists precisely in order to impose limits, set a standard of measurement that is anything but political or moral" (Ibid.).

To argue against cultural criticism, Bloom even uses "individuality," which he degrades in his previous argument, as proof of his rebuttal. Although Bloom suggests that canon excludes and eliminates unwanted or unqualified individuality strictly and unsympathetically, he still acknowledges the positive function performed by individuals in acquiring and being cultivated by the aesthetic value of canons. Individuals, as Bloom determines, are deliberately set against society. To Bloom, aesthetic is "an individual rather than societal concern" (Ibid. 16). The aesthetic value of canons is to be perceived by free-willed and "achieved individuality" (Ibid. 24). Canons are not to be diminished as subjects so easily approachable by the whole society or to yield to analysis generated from disciplines of social sciences.

Bloom's opposing voice has not yet prevented the popularity of cultural criticism and cultural studies. They have prospered to such an unexpected extent that they have attracted more interest and followers. In fact, Bloom's guardianship of the aesthetic value of canon and the classic is understandable; however, to retreat to the nostalgia of the golden old ages where canon studies remained elite and stagnant and to refuse to embrace new and alterity is not a wise gesture. To make classic studies a closed and reclusive discipline, rejecting any contribution from social sciences or cultural studies is not good for canon itself. Interdisciplinary approaches provide new perspectives for studying the classic and canon. Studies that are too limited in scope can easily be exhausted by predecessors, leaving the later generations nothing but barren fields that can no longer bear fruits. By relating and referring to other fields of studies, the classic and canon can also enjoy enduring and refreshed interest and readership.

3.5 "Centered" and "Periphery" Literatures in this Age of World Literature

Whether it is legitimate to establish a set of canon that excludes and discriminates against other literatures and cultures becomes a more urgent issue to resolve in this age of world literature. Aside from its cruel function in differentiating between individual talent and in discriminating against new disciplines, canon has also been provincially taken as a means to downgrade cultures.

Voices that spare no effort in advocating the superiority of so-called "centered culture" and the inferiority of "periphery culture" have constantly been heard in this age of world literature. Pascale Casanova, for example, emphasizes the centeredness and overwhelming influence of French literature. As Casanova explains, French literature and culture, which are claimed to be dominant and centered in this world, "radiate" their impact to the "periphery" cultures. The study of these periphery literatures is no longer based on their own cultural history or literary tradition but is reduced to finding answers to only one simple and general question: How are they related to the centered French?

Aside from the inter-relation between different literatures and cultures, Casanova notices the interaction between individual creativity and the classic, and she gives her own comments about it. She sarcastically describes how ridiculous it is that some think literary works can be individual and original. Some people, as Casanova notices, hold "the unexamined assumption that every literary work must be described as an absolute exception, a sudden, unpredictable, and isolated expression of artistic creativity" (Casanova 2). They naively suppose that "each work is seen as being unique and irreducible." It is "a perfect unity that can be measured in relation only to itself, the interpreter is obliged to contemplate the ensemble of texts that form what is called the 'history of literature' as a random succession of singularities" (Ibid.).

As Casanova proceeds with her argument, however, the fact is that a text is always related to another text; we may call this "intertextuality" today. To

Casanova, if those who indulge themselves with individuality and singularity could step out of their parochialism, they would find the "configuration to which all texts belong, that is, the totality of texts and literary and aesthetic debates with which a particular work of literature enters into relation and resonance, and which forms the true basis for its singularity, its real originality" (Ibid. 3).

Casanova's intention to emphasize such relations between literary works is not to reveal the importance of the classic and tradition but rather to prove how the centered French culture dominates and how it extends and expands its influence through time and across borders. In particular, Casanova uses part of the book *The World Republic of Letters* to explain why she attaches supreme significance to French literature, under the subtitle "Paris: The City of Literature." On one hand, as Casanova suggests, Paris "symbolized the Revolution, the overthrow of the monarchy, the invention of the rights of man" (Ibid. 24). To Casanova, Paris embodies the spirit of progress and innovation. On the other hand, Paris is "also the capital of letters, the arts, luxurious living, and fashion" (Ibid.). It inspires creativity and tolerates diversity. Such praise of Paris, as Casanova asserts, is "transnational and transhistorical" (Ibid. 27).

It is perfectly legitimate to compliment Paris for the spirit of freedom and inspiration that represents the city, but it is questionable to regard it as a superior center. Casanova suggests that Paris becomes a sacred place for those people who "demand and proclaim political independence for their homelands while at the same time inaugurate national literatures and arts" (Ibid. 31). To Casanova, it is only when people come to Paris, which is the land of inspiration, that they can initiate and develop their national literatures.

Like Casanova, another renowned scholar, Franco Moretti, also suggests a kind of interaction between "centered" culture and "periphery" culture. Borrowing ideas from disciplines such as economics and inspired by the economic phenomenon and principles, Moretti suggests that the world literary system is an "unequal" one:

I will borrow this initial hypothesis from the world-system school of economic history, for which international capitalism is a system that is simultaneously one, and unequal: with a core, and a periphery (and a semiperiphery) that are bound together in a relationship of growing inequality. One, and unequal: one literature (Weltliteratur, singular, as in Goethe and Marx), or perhaps, better, one world literary system (of inter-related literatures); but a system which is different from what Goethe and Marx had hoped for, because it's profoundly unequal. (Moretti 56)

The inter-relation between the "core" and the "periphery" culture resembles that between Prospero and Caliban in Shakespeare's *The Tempest*. Prospero always thinks himself superior and advanced. To cultivate Caliban and to teach him language, as Prospero supposes, is a generous and valid gesture. To Caliban, however, such enforced culture and cultivation is colonization rather than civilization. To Moretti, the influence of the "core culture" is so overwhelming and superior as to be rejected by the "periphery cultures," yet the "core cultures" always ignore and downgrade the "periphery."

It seems that only the "core" cultures have the right to designate canons. In addition, it is not likely for masterpieces from "periphery" cultures to gain access to this closed and exclusive list of canon determined by the aesthetic and historical values derived from the "core" cultures. The authorized canons from the "core" cultures enjoy more familiarity and readership; meanwhile, it is difficult for works from "periphery" cultures to be accepted by or introduced to a foreign audience.

But is it really valid or beneficial to have a fixed and closed set of canons decided by the "core" cultures in this age of world literature? Peter Carravetta, in his article "The Canon(s) of World Literature," suggests that "the creation of a single canon of world literature, however circumscribed, cannot realistically be construed, although critics have at different times essayed to do precisely that, inevitably starting from within one national perspective" (Carravetta 265).

The exchange and communication between different cultures and literatures has prospered to an unprecedented level in this age of world literature. Any attempt to construct barriers between borders, languages, or cultural contexts is in vain. Readers of world literature may be bred within different historical backgrounds and may be cultivated by different cultural

86 contexts; they are likely to hold distinguished perspectives and have different specialized fields of study and familiarity. Such differences, however, do not wipe out the affinities and possibilities for mutual understanding between different cultures and literatures. With such a base for cross-cultural communication, one cannot attempt to discriminate against the ability of individuals from other cultures to perceive and appreciate canons from the original culture.

At the same time, to advocate communication does not legitimate the gesture to impose a fixed and foreign list of canons on readers. Doing so will frustrate individual creativity and diversity. The interaction between cultures should be based on the fact that no culture should be discriminated against or considered to be superior or inferior. The relationship should be reciprocal from both perspectives.

The question, then, is what canon is in this age of world literature, and how canon can be read? As Carravetta suggests, the identity of world literature canons is "out to shift not to difference but to multiplicity, to hybridity, and in more practical terms, given the role of translation as an encounter, to content, to processes of assimilation, and to variable modes of relation" (Ibid. 269). To Carravetta, canons of world literature should therefore be in a state of mobility and multiplicity rather than a fixed and stagnant list of works. This reminds us of David Damrosch's definition of world literature. In his book *What Is World Literature,* Damrosch suggests that world literature should be defined as a "mode of circulation" (Damrosch, *What Is World Literature* 5). Such mobility in the concept of world literature resonates with Carravetta's idea about canons of world literature.

To further illustrate the mobility of canons in this age of world literature, Carravetta borrows two notions: the notion of "migration" and the notion of "traveling theory." By the notion of "migration," Carravetta means that canon should be considered an adaptive concept that is tolerant of diversity and differences:

> The idea is to make the inevitably censoring function of canon formation not a tool for literary ideologies of inclusion and exclusion, but rather a compass for

selected itineraries ever open to engage the texts which literally and metaphorically speak a different language, manifest forms utterly new to us, and compel a humbling self-critique. (Carravetta 270)

Such encompassing and adaptive features make the concept of canon well-received and suitable for this age of world literature. Canon is not held as measures to evaluate or to eliminate but is rather held as measures to embrace and encourage. Canon, in this sense, is more like a grand river that travels across borders, overcoming barriers and attracting and accepting contributions from either little streams that are anonymous or large rivers that enjoy national respect and represent national identity.

The notion of "traveling theory" therefore resonates with such a simile. Carravetta borrows this idea from Edward Said (Ibid. 271). The notion of "migration" may refer to a flexible and adaptive list of canons. The notion of "traveling theory," conversely, refers to the same list of canons that circulates between different contexts. Instead of forcing the target audience to interpret the same canons in some determined or authorized way, scholars should embrace different perspectives. Carravetta suggests that "issues of intertextuality, migration, and reconceptualization of any value expressed in the writing itself demand new critical approaches, a different hermeneutics of culture" (Ibid.). To contribute new perspectives to studies of canons not only makes the voices of the minor and strange heard but also makes it so that the major and traditional can be inspired and improved.

What Carravetta advocates is an open list of canons that at the same time generously receives new approaches and applauds new perspectives. Carravetta concludes his article by saying that scholars in this age of world literature should "set up a flexible methodology, and direct [their] students toward endless heterologies and possibilities of understanding, none of which is or can ever be the last word" (Ibid.). Contrary to Casanova and Moretti, Carravetta holds quite tolerant attitudes toward canons. The gesture to "open" canon will certainly facilitate circulation and communication between different cultures and literatures. To enable readers access to different kinds of excellence in literatures is a treasure and priority bestowed by this age of world literature, and to revitalize the classic and canon with new perspectives and originality benefits both the old and the forthcoming.

88   It is rewarding to hold an open attitude toward the classic and canon, and it is beneficial to boost perspectives that feature individuality and personality to approach the classic and canon. The problem, however, is that to highly emphasize the openness of canons and the classic does not mean that random and irresponsible approaches can twist and even violate the essential values that have been revealed within the classic and canon throughout time and history. We admire diversity and individuality that revitalizes the classic and canon, but we should still pay due respect to values in the classic and canon that may be traditional and old but are also essential and enduring.

Recent years have witnessed all kinds of cross-cultural communication of the classic and canon, such as adaptations of the classic works, translations of them, and appending interpretive footnotes. How to balance the classic and creativity, essentiality and diversity, is an important issue to be addressed in this age of world literature.

Chapter Four

Struggle between the Classic and Creativity in Adaptation: *The Tempest* and *A Tempest*

Anyone who adapts a piece of the classic must experience a struggle between the classic and creativity. The classic can be altered to cater for the tastes of younger generations. It can be changed to fit in with different historical contexts. It can be transformed according to personal preference or even prejudice, and it can be shortened or extended because of a deliberately selected emphasis or concealment.

The question, however, is to what extent should the classic be adapted (twisted)? Should we completely disregard and deny the value embedded within a piece of the classic and regenerate it? Should we treat the classic as inexhaustible sources of bouncing but random ideas and subject them to free but irresponsible and unreasonable adaptation without due respect and appreciation? Or should we leave the classic to be ghettoized by the biased perspective that overwhelms them because of a certain popular adaptation and causes the classic to lose their original shape and become obsolete?

Because of the renaissance of world literature, this age witnesses the prosperity of communication between different cultures, regardless of the geographical distance, political borders, or lingual barriers. The classic is circulated and introduced between and within different cultures; this attracts different responses, inspires competing ideas, and provokes diverse feelings. People from different cultural backgrounds may produce different perspectives about alien classics; thus, the initiative and demand to create adaptations is prompted. Different preferences, emphases, and feelings within the adaptations are expressed, some of which may be biased and partial. To understand and respect different perspectives is to be advocated, but to prioritize and worship the local perspective within an adaption and ghettoize a certain piece of the classic by rigidly adhering to a single perspective seems to derail from the trend of diversity that is appreciated in this age of world literature. In this chapter, I take Shakespeare's classic play *The Tempest* and Aimer Cesaire's adaptation of the play, *A Tempest,* to argue against the ghettoization of the classic and cultures in this age of world literature.

4.1 Transformation and Ghettoization of *The Tempest*

On January 14, 2012, an article entitled "Who's Afraid of *The Tempest*?" appeared on the news website *Salon*. It reported on a ban on ethnic studies in Arizona, a state in the United States. The ban resulted in the proscription of "Mexican-American history, local authors and even Shakespeare" (Biggers). Shakespeare's classic play *The Tempest* is involved. It seems that *The Tempest* is no less intimidating than a real tempest. The prompted debates and provoked feelings can be more intense than a roaring storm. Whether *The Tempest* conveys a sense of discrimination against "the other" has been drawing enduring controversy and has become a major public concern when studying and circulating this classic play.

Interestingly, the trouble encountered by *The Tempest* reminds us of Caliban's accusation of Prospero's teaching:

> Miranda: Abhorred slave,
>
> Which any print of goodness wilt not take,
>
> Being capable of all ill! I pitied thee,

Took pains to make thee speak, taught thee each hour

...

Caliban: You taught me language; and my profit on't

Is, I know how to curse. The red plague rid you

For learning me your language! (Shakespeare 33).

What is in Prospero's view the symbol of cultivation, the language, has become Caliban's weapon to curse. Cursing, as the most indecent and negative function of the various functions of language, has been acquired and recognized by Caliban as the only function. The classic, which is supposed to nourish domestic readers as well as foreign readers, is regarded as intimidating and in urgent need of removal. Due to the one particular assumption that it is a text about racial discrimination, *The Tempest,* which consists of far more than one aspect of interpretation, has been labeled and determined as a piece of work that must be restricted to postcolonial readings. It is unfair for us to blame Shakespeare for his alleged racial discrimination without his in-person defense, but how to interpret the classic is indeed a problem that is of essential importance.

The question is how *The Tempest* has been transformed from a literary classic into a banned book? How to understand Shakespeare's *The Tempest* seems to be more an issue of history than of literary studies. The interpretation of it has always been subjected to new findings or evidence of history. In an article named "*The Tempest* Transformed," the authors trace back the history of the play's transformation and try to align different interpretations with their particular contexts so as to better reveal how and why it has been transformed (Vaughan and Vaughan 1). The article reveals that the reason why *The Tempest* has been transformed into a text reserved for colonial studies may be attributed to new discourse findings or geographical evidence that are related to specific historical events, such as sea explorations or a shipwreck.

Dating back to 1808, Edmond Malone published a pamphlet entitled *An Account of the Incidents from Which the Title and Part of the Story of Shakespeare's Tempest Were Derived and Its True Date Ascertained*, in which "he reviewed the reports on the 1609 storms and voyagers caught in it, in an effort to make apparent why he believed this particular storm inspired Shakespeare to write *The Tempest*" (Stritmatter and Kositsky 5). He insists that Shakespeare must have read about "one or more of the several descriptions that appeared in London in 1610 and 1611 of the Gates-Somers expedition's shipwreck on Bermuda in 1609" (Vaughan and Vaughan 5), and with this assertion he concludes that *The Tempest* must be about "English imperialism." Although "subsequent editors and critics generally acknowledged tangential ties between the pamphlets and the play," in the nineteenth century, this claim managed to gain acknowledgment from the majority of English and American scholars, who "contend that Shakespeare meant *The Tempest* to be substantially about English imperialism, to take place in English America (perhaps even in Bermuda)" (Ibid.).

"Shakespeare meant *The Tempest* to be substantially about English imperialism." Such a declarative statement seems persuasive and pervasive, as it seems to be supported by genuine evidence from the pamphlets, and it enjoys cross-continental approval. Moreover, under such a claim, everything can be accounted with perfect logic: The oversea venture occurred during Shakespeare's time; the destination of Bermuda was English American, which was colonized by Shakespeare's home country; as a renowned and representative citizen, Shakespeare was highly expected to be exposed to such news and sources and must have read about the overseas venture and shared opinions with the pamphlets, which were very likely written by his courageous compatriots. With such an assertion, Shakespeare's depiction of Caliban as cruel and savage is justifiably condemned because of the assumption that he feels superior as part of the country that exports colonization.

Things grow wilder. The influence of this claim persisted in the twentieth century. The validity of the claim was no longer guaranteed by the necessary historical facts, nor did the authorial intention matter any more, because "what matters to many twentieth century interpreters are the power relations between the colonizer and the colonized that seem embedded in the play's plot and characters" (Ibid. 6). The play seemed to be detached from any assumed geographical or chronological context but became an independent and representative work ready for "still broader geographic and symbolic applications" (Ibid.).

Aime Cesaire's *A Tempest*, an adapted play from *The Tempest,* was produced under this circumstance. In 1969, Aime Cesaire, a Martinique-born politician who had made consistent efforts in the revolt against colonization, rewrote the story and titled it *A Tempest*. The adapted play was intended to be performed for black audiences in particular. Although the plots of the original play were preserved, the style of language and the features of the characters were modified. Richard Miller, the translator of Cesaire's *A Tempest* from French to English, mentioned that Cesaire "denied any attempting any linguistic echo of Shakespeare" (Cesaire, *A Tempest* II). Caliban, the most targeted figure among scholars of colonial studies, is also depicted differently in *A Tempest*. Unlike the cruel and uncivilized Caliban in Shakespeare's *The Tempest*, he is featured in *A Tempest* as "a hero through the illumination of his culture," brave and with integrity. Such a shift in Caliban's personality, as the comment of the book suggests, is "perhaps the most significant accomplishment of *A Tempest*" (Ibid.). Considering Cesaire's political standpoint, it is not unexpected that he intends to depict Caliban as an upstanding fighter revolting against the evil invasion of the colonizers. Cesaire, in his book *Discourse on Colonialism,* argues that it is unreasonable and pretentious to justify colonization by describing its purpose as importing civilization to the "primitive" land. He declares that "between colonization and civilization there is an infinite distance." He severely condemns the cruelty of colonization, calling it not having "a single human value" (Cesaire, *Discourse on Colonialism* 2). *A Tempest* adopts a different perspective, reverses the roles, and provides a rebuttal against *The Tempest*, which, under these circumstances, is regarded as a piece of the classic that portrays racial discrimination.

The gesture to reduce *The Tempest* to a work about colonization and to interpret the classic with this exclusive perspective certainly prompts opposing voices. In his article, "Stormy Weather: Misreading the Postcolonial Tempest," Peter Hulme (who defends the validity of approaching *The Tempest* from the angle of colonial studies) quotes some of the scholars who have criticized and interrogated this way of thinking. Brian Vickers, for example, is one of the critics who fire fierce criticism against the colonial perspective and guard the orthodox and traditional way of appreciating Shakespeare

94 in books such as *Appropriating Shakespeare*, which obviously means to read Shakespeare appropriately and, more importantly, to revise the derailed or distorted interpretations. Vickers's accusation about the postcolonial reading of *The Tempest* is relentless. Hulme paraphrases Vickers's opinion and suggests that "according to Vickers, postcolonial readings of *The Tempest* are guilty of reducing the play to 'an allegory about colonialism' with Prospero seen as 'an exploitative protocapitalist' and Caliban 'an innocent savage, deprived of his legitimate heritage'" (Hulme). Vickers's disagreement with these critics is also strong and severe: He asserts that they "have leftish pretensions and therefore tend to see capitalists or protocapitalists in any figure that wields authority, and they are incurably romantic about the Third World and will therefore sentimentalize all natives" (qtd. in Hulme). To Vickers, the postcolonial reading of *The Tempest* is less an alternative perspective to approach the play than "a kind of show-trial in which works of literature, amongst them *The Tempest*, are judged in the balance and found guilty of endorsing colonialism and its evils" (Ibid.).

Another kind of critique, as Hulme suggests, is "to try to construct a third position, above or beyond the conflict." Jonathan Bate is one of the scholars who embrace "pluralism" in interpreting *The Tempest*. Interspersed in Hulme's paraphrases and quotations from Bate are sarcastic comments made by Hulme. Hulme suggests that by emphasizing the "capriciousness" of Shakespeare's work, Bate cunningly devised a scheme for "evolving and mutating" the classic play to "cope with changing cultural environments" (Hulme). To Bate, although a "Prosperian" reading dominates, the alternative "Calibanesque" reading "has always been latent in the play" (qtd. in Hulme). He elevates Shakespeare's work to a level where it is "not just an icon of various European nationhoods but a voice of what we now call multiculturalism" (Ibid.). Hulme ironically points out that Bate's idea is "in the classically liberal fashion," a situation with conflicting and paradoxical trends (Hulme). Bate neither denies the contribution of new perspectives, as he gives "weight to the powerful readings and rewritings offered of *The*

Tempest," nor downplays the value of the classic, as he argues "that all these readings have somehow been locked up in the play waiting for Frantz Fanon to come along and liberate them" (Ibid.).

4.2 Particularity and Diversity Indicated by *A Tempest*

In fact, if we look at one of the "Calibanesque" versions of the classic play, Cesaire's *A Tempest*, we may find it resonates with this kind of "pluralism" reading. Cesaire's political intention to fight against colonialism stands out in *A Tempest,* and his Caliban has indeed served as a qualified utterer of such voices. Although these characteristics of *A Tempest* biasedly restrict and reduce *The Tempest* to a monotonous focus on anti-colonialism, there are elements that contribute to the sense of multiplicity and diversity that is due to the classic's "universality." Shakespeare's *The Tempest,* with the definite article "the," seems to depict a particular tempest within which a specific event happened. The title resembles that of a documentary recording a devastating storm in history. Cesaire, conversely, displaced the definite article with the indefinite article "a" in *A Tempest*, in a deliberate gesture to prepare readers for a fabricated story or a tale under such a title. In fact, Cesaire may intend *A Tempest* to be more of an alternative in interpreting the classic than a contrast against it. It attempts to parallel or even challenge the authority of the classic by adopting an alternative perspective to reveal a different version of the story. In fact, Cesaire not only means the play to show alterity; he prefaces the adapted play with a prelude in which he indicates the indefinite feature of the original meaning of a work and thus the possibility of diverse and multiple "alternatives."

The prelude begins with a narrator's voice contextualizing the play within a live theatre. Following this are the words of a "Master of Ceremonies" directing readers' attention to the backstage and disclosing what happened behind the curtain and before the play:

Ambiance of a psychodrama. The actors enter singly, at random, and each chooses for himself a mask at his leisure (Cesaire, A *Tempest* 1).

MASTER OF CEREMONIES: Come gentlemen, help yourselves. To each his character, to each character his mask. You, Prospero? Why not? He has reserves of will power he's not even aware of himself. You want Caliban? Well, that's revealing. Ariel? Fine with me. And what about Stephano, Trinculo? No Takers? Ah, just in time! It takes all kinds to make a world (Ibid.).

Normally in psychodramas, as Peter Felix Kellermann suggests in his book *Focus on Psychodrama: Therapeutic Aspects of Psychodrama*, "participants are invited to reenact significant experiences and to present their subjective worlds with the aid of a group" (Kellermann 11); however, "the reenactments are as different from each other as are the lives of the people who present them" (Ibid. 12). Thus, by situating the play within the "ambiance of a psychodrama," Cesaire indicates the personal and subjective feature of the acting in the play. By contextualizing the play as having the "ambiance of a psychodrama," Cesaire discredits the story told in *The Tempest* as nothing more than a mere dream with a shaky or even non-existent link to truth or history. The presentation of the same character by different actors with various life experiences and perspectives can be dramatically diverse. As Cesaire suggests in the prelude, the allocation of characters within the acting crew is "at random" and "at leisure." It is possible that the play could be another version if the set of characters were assigned differently. By describing how the "Master" allocates the characters so randomly and casually to actors and by referring to the characters as just "masks" to be worn by actors, Cesaire again deconstructs the seriousness of *The Tempest* and shows that it is just acting that makes up the story rather than the real people behind it who react to the historical event. It is subjective and pretend rather than objective and true. These indefinite characteristics of the play certainly differentiate it from the definite and objective historical events. Cesaire's intention to question and undermine the authoritativeness of *The Tempest* is obvious. By doing so, Cesaire reduces *The Tempest* to a mere illusion that needs not be taken as seriously as it has been. The audience, then, are intrigued to ask how much truth can be derived from a play such as *The Tempest,* which is assumed to be historically based.

Although it is a work developed from the postcolonial reading, *A Tempest* with such features is less likely to be approved by Peter Hulme. In his article "Nymphs and Reapers," Hulme expresses his concern about detaching the literary work from the moment of textual production and deconstructing the original meaning. To Hulme, "*The Tempest* read by Sir Walter Raleigh in 1914 as the work of England's national poet is very different from *The Tempest* constructed with full textual apparatus by an editor/ critic such as Frank Kermode" (Barker and Hulme 195). That "different but contemporaneous inscriptions take place," however, as Hulme warns, "should not lead inescapably to the point where the only option becomes the voluntaristic ascription to the text of meanings and articulations derived simply from one's own ideological preferences" (Ibid. 196). The outcome of this can be as devastating as that of the claim about "the capriciousness of Shakespeare's work" and "pluralism reading," as Hulme suggests that "this is a procedure only too vulnerable to pluralistic incorporation, a recipe for peaceful coexistence with the dominant readings, not for a contestation of those readings themselves" (Hulme). The result of the contestation, as Hulme points out, is certainly that "the postcolonial readings of *The Tempest* are not better just because they tend to be more interesting," but "they both read the play better, and read the misreadings of others" (Ibid.).

It seems that Hulme not only argues for the validity of the postcolonial reading of *The Tempest* but also strives to make it exclusive and dominant, displacing rather than paralleling the traditional reading of it. If the postcolonial reading of *The Tempest* becomes the single approach to the play and is emphasized too much over other perspectives, the fate of the classic play is not very promising, considering the ban on it in Arizona. Should we insist on and guard the supreme and exclusive authority of a perspective, disregarding the situation where the classic gradually becomes obsolete? Should we deprive the following generations of the classic, whose value was originally recognized and lasting? In this age of world literature, where the travelling of the classic works between cultures and beyond borders is becoming more frequent and common, the questions are becoming more complicated. Should we confine the classic to a specific contextual environment and ghettoize it within the particular historical background? Or should we completely detach the classic from their origins and deliberately sacrifice and twist their meaning and features to cater for diverse demands and different preferences?

4.3 Deconstruct the Postcolonial Reading of *The Tempest*

As it is impossible for scholars to ask Shakespeare in person about his authorial intent, critics rely on assumption and imagination to relate the interpretation of the work to the biographical and contextual facts, as long as they correspond logically. They may also coordinate different discoveries from different times and places to make up sound and convincible explanations of a certain piece of work so as to cater for the fashion of their own age. They could extend the fabrication so far that they may even disregard the already shaky facts, creating new layers of meanings, which are nothing but subjective. In the case of *The Tempest*, three questions need to be asked. Is it fair to determine that *The Tempest* is only a text for postcolonial studies because of an assumption that Shakespeare read the pamphlets "recording" the English overseas venture? Is it possible that it is criticism shaped within a particular context that creates the meaning of colonialism in *The Tempest*? Is it possible that *The Tempest* has been reduced to a mere symbol of power relations advocated by a society of a certain age?

In fact, the postcolonial reading of the classic play *The Tempest* is not undeniable or indisputable. Upon careful consideration, it can be deconstructed. Historical facts, which are regarded as the consolidated grounds of the postcolonial reading, boost postcolonial specialists' confidence in claiming the priority of the perspective. Yet History is not always reliable. What we call "facts" can be subjectively fabricated instead of objectively factual. The unreliability of history has been discussed in different cultures throughout time. In Chinese history, for example, the untruth of history is attributed to human beings' involvement in passing on historical facts. In Chinese courts during ancient times, positions such as Official of History were established and assigned. This entitlement allowed them to record history. In his preface to the book *Truth and History — The History Thoughts and Ethnic Compassion of Fu Sinian and Chen Yinque*, Luo Zhitian reveals the divergence in ways to pass on history in China: to record and to write (Schneider 5). The distinction between the two is as obvious as the literal meanings on the surface. To record seems to be less subjective, as it is subject to the original being of the historical facts with the least human involvement. To write, however, indicates the possibility of the deliberate fabrication and creation of human beings added to the historical facts or stories. Although the former sounds more objective, Luo sharply points out that it still cannot escape completely from human beings' manipulation. The purpose of recording, the selective process of determining what is to be recorded, and the way and tone in which certain historical facts are recorded are all dependent on humans' personal and diverse behaviors (Ibid.). To avoid subjectivity when dealing with history is infeasible; this is also evidenced by the case of Fu Sinian, whose attempt to institutionalize history studies as a discipline of science with absolutely objective evidence ultimately became an irritating dilemma (Ibid.). Therefore, even if the historical events of the sea ventures actually happened and the existence of the pamphlets is material evidence, the connection made between them and Shakespeare's *The Tempest* is subjective and deliberate. Understandable as it is to attribute Caliban's savage-like behavior to the anecdotes recorded in the venture pamphlets, such a connection is not a final determinant in concluding that Shakespeare meant to prioritize it as the only reflection of the play.

The history-oriented approach contributes to the postcolonial label of *The Tempest*, which, as the above discussion suggests, requires second thoughts. There are other reasons that may account for *The Tempest* being reduced to a text for colonial studies; these other reasons are also in desperate need of examination. As it is difficult for us to determine and verify Shakespeare's authorial intention, the criticism that emerged afterward can determine the direction of our study on the classic play. Oscar Wilde, in one of his critical articles "The Critic as Artist," argues that artistic creativity is attributable to criticism. He denies the priority of artistic creativity but deifies criticism, which in his view regenerates and revitalizes the former. To history, he attaches no due seriousness as historicists do, but he treats it as something that can be and should be revisable. Although they are given in the form of conversation with witty expressions, these ideas do not appear to be any less bombarding than those that take the form of formal argumentations. To further demonstrate these ideas, several paragraphs that are particularly concerned with the superiority of criticism over creativity have been selected and are listed here:

> Gilbert: Each new school, as it appears, cries out against criticism, but it is to the critical faculty in man that it owes its origin. The mere creative instinct does not innovate, but reproduce. (Wilde, *The Importance of Being Earnest* 250)
>
> Gilbert: I am aware that there are many honest workers in painting as well as in literature who object to criticism entirely. They are quite right. Their work stands in no intellectual relation to their age. It brings us no new element of pleasure. It suggests no fresh departure of thought, or passion, or beauty. It should not be spoken of. It should be left to the oblivion that it deserves. (Wilde, *Collected Works of Oscar Wilde* 978)
>
> Ernest: Gilbert, you treat the world as if it were a crystal ball. You hold it in your hand and reverse it to please a willful fancy. You do nothing but re-write history. (Ibid. 979)
>
> Gilbert: The one duty we owe to history is to re-write it. (Ibid.)

To Wilde, art is the reproduction of criticism. The question, however, is from what should criticism originate? Criticism, as Wilde indicates in the third paragraph listed above, should be attributed to the intellectual trends of the living generation. Art that rejects criticism, as Wilde suggests, should be accused of having "no intellectual relation to [its] age" (Ibid. 978). Having nothing new or fresh either to fit in with the present age or to further stimulate and inspire new thoughts in the future, the art is destined to be obsolete and forgotten. History, as Wilde believes, is like a "crystal ball" that requires the constant changing of angles to enable the holders to see different or even reversed views, preserving little of the old picture to remain fanciful to the present holder and securing utility for the contemporary age. Therefore, Wilde comes to the startling conclusion given in the above quoted paragraph: "The one duty we owe to history is to re-write it" (Ibid. 979).

Another perspective that may explain the popularity and domination of the postcolonial reading of *The Tempest* is the "power relations" represented and illuminated in Michel Foucault's article "What is an Author." Its overrated influence on function in determining the meaning of the classic should be re-examined. In this article, Foucault incisively points out that not only is the discourse itself deprived of the need to be closely read, but the author's intention is also disregarded and dismissed, as the author's name is

> unlike other proper names, which moves from the interior of a discourse to the real person outside who produced it, the name of the author remains at the contours of texts — seperating one from the other, defining their form and characterizing their mode of existence. (Foucault 123).

What matters is the position that people assign to the discourse. This will represent its function to the utmost within the power relations of a society or a community, and it will serve as an indispensable link to guarantee the smooth operation of the power system, as Foucault diagnoses that "the function of an author is to characterize the existence, circulation and operation of certain discourses within a society" (Ibid. 124). If we refer to *The Tempest*, critics' declaration of the singularity of the postcolonial reading of *The Tempest* caters to the emerging and prevailing concerns about colonialism and postcolonialism in the nineteenth and twentieth centuries, contributing the consistent discovery to the new trends of the time. *The Tempest* has become a literary demonstrator and discourse evidence of the heatedly discussed topic of power relations between colonizers and the colonized.

The transformation of *The Tempest* as a label only for postcolonial reading has thus been accomplished. Just as Hulme argues against the traditional interpretations, most of which are renaissance-concerned and humanistic-oriented, scholars have tried to revitalize the seemingly oblivious classic, endowing it with new tastes and perspectives of colonial studies. In addition, just as Wilde predicts how the school of art comes into being courtesy of criticism, colonial studies of *The Tempest* were indeed established as a new school of study when the transformation of *The Tempest* into a text for colonial studies was widely accepted and approved in the twentieth century. It is to cater for and make the play fit in with the fashion of the time, colonial studies, by reducing *The Tempest* into a mere symbol of the power relations between the colonizer and the colonized, precisely in the way Foucault anticipates that the discourse will be sacrificed and altered due to the demands of time.

Unlike Hulme, who claims the postcolonial reading to be the only reading and the exclusive reading, we recognize the value in the above three aspects and do not disregard them completely. The historical approach encourages us to find the real cultural background of the play. Creative criticism inspires and stimulates new perspectives, and the angle of power relations may reveal a different perspective that we have not realized or adopted to analyze more specific problems. What should be remembered here is that no approach is so perfect and definite that it can attach a sole form of interpretation to a piece of the classic while at the same time invalidating the others. The introduction to the book *Critical Essays on Shakespeare's The Tempest* presents similar ideas when it reaches its conclusion after outlining the transformation of *The Tempest*. Although perspectives of *The Tempest* prosper, "they offer no definitive closure, no universally acceptable perspective. Nor can they be taken as predictive of *The Tempest*'s future" (Vaughan and Vaughan 12). *The Tempest* is "one of Shakespeare's richest and most engaging dramas" and embraces "multiple avenues" in its interpretations (Ibid.). Such attitudes are needed when reading the classic, and the universality of the classic deserves recognition and respect. To achieve such goals, one must be equipped with the sensitivity to feel the multiple perspectives that potentially exist, with the tolerance to acknowledge their necessity, and with the capability to understand them. Thus, when dealing with a piece of the classic works, the ideal method is to make the different perspectives complement each other rather than contrast with each other. The different perspectives should not devalue or even deny one another's validity in interpreting the classic.

4.4 Universality and Multiple Perspectives of the Classic

As we have discussed in previous parts, Bate's argument about the "capriciousness" of Shakespeare, which Hulme ironically rebutted, may find support from T. S. Eliot's idea about the classic. In his address "What Is a Classic," which was "delivered before the Virgil Society," Eliot reminds us of the attributes that determine the value of the classic: "variety," "comprehensiveness," and "relatedness." "Variety," as Eliot elucidates, refers to the potential of the classic to be approached from interdisciplinary perspectives and its quality to inspire intellectual minds from different specialized fields. Virgil's work, for example, as Eliot asserts, is so inclusive that "no specialized knowledge or proficiency can confer the exclusive title to talk about Virgil" (Eliot, "What Is a Classic" 7). The inclusiveness of Virgil's classic work can break through the boundaries between different subjects and reach different individuals, as "each can give his testimony of Virgil in relation to those subjects which he knows best, or upon which he has most deeply reflected: that is what I meant by variety" (Ibid.). The fact that the classic can arouse people's empathy regardless of their conditions reflects another characteristic of the classic, and that is "comprehensiveness." The classic works, as Eliot argues, "express the maximum possible of the whole range of feeling which represents the character of the people who speak that language" (Ibid. 27). They "represent this at its best" and "have the widest appeal" (Ibid.). The classic is able to impress on and resonate with people's minds. Diverse feelings and responses are prompted and expected from readers.

The classic, as Eliot observes, reaches beyond the monolingual environment. The other feature of the classic, defined by Eliot as "relatedness," refers to the classic's significance in cross-cultural communications. According to Eliot, to be aware of and to appreciate the excellence of other cultures represents the progress and elevation of one's civilization. Virgil, as Eliot suggests, "was constantly adapting and using the discoveries, traditions and inventions of Greek poetry," and "it is this development of one literature, or civilization, in relation to another, which gives a peculiar significance to the subject of Virgil's epic" (Ibid. 19). This idea about "relatedness" elaborated by Eliot can be another enlightening reference to support the validity of world literature prospering today. That the classic from different backgrounds circulate and communicate beyond lingual or national borders reflects a kind of reciprocal relationship between different cultures. As Eliot suggests, "to make use of a foreign literature in this way marks a further stage of civilization beyond making use only of the earlier stages of one's own" (Ibid.).

The truth is that such "relatedness" is by no means a simple practice of talking about the foreign within the domestic; it is more of a humble confession that admits the inevitable impact of the precedent culture and more of an active learning and borrowing of its prosperity into the domestic works. Such worship is neither a symbol of inferiority of the present to the precedent, nor a symbol of repression of the domestic by the foreign. Rather, it is a sign of progress. It is exactly the humble consciousness of others' influences and the modest acquisition of their excellence that distinguishes the present and the domestic. Eliot conveys such ideas by expressing his preference for the Roman over the Greek, stating that "this is a consciousness which the Romans had, and which the Greeks, however much more highly we may estimate their achievement — and indeed, we may respect it all the more on this account — could not possess" (Ibid.).

To Eliot, the classic is academically, emotionally, and culturally inclusive. If we borrow Eliot's ideas and apply them to the case of *The Tempest* and *A Tempest*, the conclusion reached may diverge from Hulme's insights about the relationship between these two pieces of literary work. Postcolonial studies, as a specialized field, can certainly produce possible and provoking perspectives to interpret Shakespeare's *The Tempest*; however, the perspectives from this one specialized discipline cannot claim to be exclusive or exhaustive. Opposing voices and negative feelings prompted by the classic play are also to be expected and reasonable. The various and polemical responses extend the life of the classic work and reflect the inexhaustible feature of it, and there should be no hierarchy between different feelings and opinions. The play reaches beyond the domestic context and relates to foreign cultures. Not only does it boost communication between the two contexts behind the two literary works, but this communication also benefits both as they exchange perspectives to inform and perceive the event. To trace the play back to its historical context and moment of creation and to be faithful to it certainly counts as serious scholarship, but Hulme's insistence on taking the postcolonial viewpoint of *The Tempest* as the only authentic and the best perspective does not seem to be so justified. To rigidly adhere to the pamphlet that records the historical tempest as the only source of the play and deliberately disregard or deny the possibility of other historical, cultural, or textual impacts upon the creation of the literary work frustrates studies of *The Tempest*.

The idea about the universality of the classic may also find support from Nietzsche's arguments in *On the Genealogy of Morals,* where he talks about the concept of "perspectivism." To Nietzsche, the absolute and ultimate "reason" or "objectivity" is nothing but an illusion (Nietzsche, *On the Genealogy of Morals* 98). There is no essential meaning within a literary work that can transcend or overcome differences in time and space, nor is there any common sense of a work that can be simultaneously approved among different subjectivities. The meaning of a certain work arises from different perspectives. Perspective determines the meaning. Therefore, a work can be universal in the sense that every perspective can find correspondence resonating within the classic. This sounds similar to the features of "variety" and "comprehensiveness" elaborated by Eliot in "What Is a Classic," which suggest that the classic is disciplinarily and emotionally resonating.

Nietzsche's idea, however, is somewhat relativist and pessimistic. Although he acknowledges the coexistence of different perspectives and their validity in determining interpretations, he negates the fact that there is absolute and ultimate "reason" or "objectivity" in the classic on which those perspectives are based and from which those perspectives are developed. It seems to Nietzsche that the classic is constantly experiencing metamorphoses and works therein lose their roots; however, what is fundamental may not necessarily be an abstract essence, the origin and existence of which Nietzsche denies. There are thematic questions within the classic that can transcend time, space, and different subjectivities and that are understandable and communicable beyond lingual, national, and cultural borders. Zhang Longxi, in his article "The Poetics of World Literature," argues that "we may define the poetics of world literature as a set of fundamental questions about nature, qualities, values, and components of literature so understood, rather than an infinite, ungraspable conglomeration of all the critical views in the world's different traditions" (Zhang Longxi, "The Poetics of World Literature" 356). Rather than an uncoordinated and unregulated mixture of perspectives, there are focused and fundamental elements within the classic that root, inspire, and retrieve and integrate perspectives.

These fundamental questions are the very determinants that ensure the consistency and constancy of the classic transcending through time, place, and subjectivity. They contribute to the universality of the classic, which makes the transcendence of them feasible and reasonable. In *Karmic Traces*, as previously discussed, Weinberger notices and describes how poems regardless of their different contexts manage to transcend time and space: "The poet dies, the biographical facts are lost, and the poem remains. The language changes, meanings drop out, and the poem remains. The language is no longer spoken, the city in which it was written is a buried ruin, and the poem remains" (Weinberger 156).

The unchangeable and indestructible power that preserves the poem is indeed derived from the fundamental questions to which it alludes. Fundamental questions such as issues concerning nature, quality, and value are always the major concerns of different times, regardless of their different contextual backgrounds and different subjectivities. The motive and interest in discussing these questions are never dimmed or extinguished. Thus, the classic is perpetuated as reliable and rewarding references because the classic, within which fundamental issues are discussed, is always helpful and inspiring for later generations. Moreover, the perceptibility and understandability of such questions are universal. Either predecessors or contemporaries are able to participate in discussions about these fundamental issues. It is not surprising when Weinberger jokes in a similar sentence pattern as Jane Austen's beginning sentence in *Pride and Prejudice* that "it is nearly a universal belief, among poets, that someone else writes what they write" (Ibid. 154). Although the blossom of different perspectives contributes and reflects the inexhaustibleness of the classic, the perspectives should never be rootless or unreasonably relative. The prosperity of perspectives and the passionate and polemical discussion that has endured through time, space, and subjectivity should be traced back to the fundamental questions that deserve constant examination and reflection.

Perspectives and fundamental questions are two attributes of the classic that complement rather than contrast with each other. The ideal way to study and extend the life and liveliness of the classic is to recognize the coexistence as well as the individual value of different perspectives while at the same time never letting the fundamental questions fade or be neglected. This reminds us of Eliot's introduction to a "common style" in his speech "What Is a Classic." "Common style," contrary to its literal meaning, as Eliot illustrates, is by no means the indistinguishable style that prevails and is enjoyed among excellent writers and that should be followed and implemented. It is rather "a community of taste" that embraces "refined and subtle" differences (Eliot, "What Is a Classic" 13). "A community of taste," as the passage suggests, refers exactly to elements such as fundamental questions that ground the prosperity of perspectives. Differences are "refined and subtle" in the sense that they have been consciously regulated and polished by those fundamental questions while at the same time enabling scholars to derive multiple perspectives from which to approach the classic.

The perspective of anti-colonialism through which *A Tempest* refers back to *The Tempest* can be regarded as one possible and profound interpretation of *The Tempest*. Although we question its validity by discussing the reliability of history, the creativity of criticism, and the need to incorporate power relations, we welcome and anticipate the questioned aspects of the postcolonial reading to be answered, supplemented, and illuminated by other perspectives. The over-emphasis on the postcolonial reading and the deliberate exclusion of other perspectives renders *The Tempest* parochial and provincial. We embrace and understand with empathy such a perspective, but we should never let it be definite and final so as to neglect or even negate other potential interpretations, which may be no less profound, rewarding, or inspiring. Acknowledging and welcoming the difference while at the same time never forgetting to pay due respect to the commonality that makes it possible is ideal when reading and studying the classic. Just like what Virginia Mason Vaughan and Alden T. Vaughan predict and conclude after introducing and examining the odyssey of transformation undergone by Shakespeare's *The Tempest*, "the complex metamorphoses and transformations surveyed in this introduction prove that Shakespeare's *Tempest* remains strikingly resilient, a continuing source of artistic appreciation and interpretation" (Vaughan and Vaughan 11). The classic play, as we infer from these words, "will remain open to interpretations" (Ibid.).

Yet to overwhelm the postcolonial reading of *The Tempest* with pure blame seems unfair. It is understandable for *A Tempest* to utter different voices, and it is too severe a requisite for it to be comprehensive of all perspectives and to be critical at the same time. What Cesaire needs to facilitate and enhance his position and support for the colonized is a fierce contrast against the assumed superiority of colonizers reflected in *The Tempest*. A comprehensive view may weaken his emphasis and result in impotent arguments. To make his position clear and pronounced, he may sacrifice other points or feelings that may be of more potentiality. Eliot, in his speech "What Is a Classic," also touches upon the necessity of sacrifice. He illustrates such ideas through the analysis of Alexander Pope's poetry. Although Pope's poetry reaches the highest level of English literature, as Eliot asserts, his age can neither be wholly discredited nor overestimated for the reason that "the realization of the classical qualities by Pope was obtained at a high price — to the exclusion of some greater potentialities" and "the sacrifice of some potentialities in order to realize others, is a condition of artistic creation" (Eliot, "What Is a Classic" 17).

Nevertheless, there are extremes that should be avoided when weighing up the potential perspectives of the classic. If one indulges too much in one perspective and becomes blind to the other shining points of a work, the one who Eliot calls the "specialist" may sacrifice "too much for too little" (Ibid.). If the specialist were too obstinate to admit anything other than his or her specialized area and he or she refused to step out of his or her comfort zone, he or she would be so pathetic as to have nothing to sacrifice (Ibid.). When dealing with *The Tempest*, then, should we ask the question of whether the colonialism to which *A Tempest* points is more worthy than other interpretations of *The Tempest*?

Is it so involved in its feelings of hatred and hospitality that it may lead to an over-interpretation or even misinterpretation of *The Tempest*?

The classic is universal. To determine their meaning through one particular response is parochial and provincial. *Provincial* in Eliot's speech "What Is a Classic" delivers a severer sense than the dictionary definition. Rather than "narrow in thought, in culture, in creed," which has been joked about as a slippery definition by Eliot, what he means by *provincial* is "a distortion of values, the exclusion of some, the exaggeration of others, which springs, not from lack of wide geographical perambulation, but from applying standards acquired within a limited area, to the whole of the human experience" (Ibid. 30).

It is not the distance between Martinique and England that results in the provincial understanding of *The Tempest*, nor is it the difference in their languages. The right to voice different opinions should not be oppressed, nor should efforts to have the voice heard be condemned. We should be careful to be neither parochial nor provincial, to let no exaggeration of some perspectives outshine other rewarding ones within a piece of the classic, and to let no unnecessary or unwise sacrifice ever be made.

4.5 De-Ghettoize the Classic and Culture in this Age of World Literature

How to read and study the classic and tradition and how to relate and apply them to new creations in this age of world literature are questions that await and attract discussion. To ghettoize and confine the development of literature within a specific culture seems to be an unpopular side to stand with when circulation and communication between different cultures prosper on the world literature stage. In his article "What Is World Poetry," Stephen Owen discusses a kind of "world poetry" that is completely detached from national history and traditions. He quotes several passages from Bei Dao's poems in his poetry collection *The August Sleepwalker*, one of which is "An End or a Beginning." Owen quotes Boonie MacDougall's translation of Bei Dao's poem collection *The August Walker*:

> Ah, my beloved land
> Why don't you sing any more
> Can it be true that even the ropes of the Yellow River towmen
> Like sundered lute-strings
> Reverberate no more
> True that time, this dark mirror
> Has also turned its back on you forever
> Leaving only stars and drifting clouds behind. (Bei Dao 63)

Owen expresses his strong disapproval of poems like this. Owen considers this poem to be too sentimental, which "was one of the consequences of the deceptive promise of immediacy and purity in the new poetry" (Owen, "What Is World Poetry" 30). Meanwhile, Owen argues that the modern Chinese poetry to which Bei Dao's poems belong employs "circumscribed 'local color'" and "universal images" that are "readily translatable" and "give the international reader an altogether safe and quick experience of another culture" (Ibid. 28). To Owen, such poems denote "a sense of cultural loss and decline" (Ibid. 30). They certainly betray "the glories of traditional poetry" in China (Ibid.). National literature and original tradition, as Owen indicates, are essential to world literature. It is national and cultural specificity that orient world literature and keep it from being lost in pure "uncertainty" (Ibid. 28). To Owen, letting national literature be overwhelmed by the overemphasized generality or universality of world literature is a tragic thing. As Owen points out, however, such detachment from the original culture reduces the poems to "an intricate shape on a blank background without frontiers, a shape that undergoes metamorphoses" (Ibid. 32); through constant metamorphoses, the poems merge into the target culture and lose their origin.

It seems that Owen considers Chinese culture and literature to be in a closed circle, fencing off any external influence and change. New entries should inherit and be consistent with the tradition and the classic within the circle. The ghettoization of the Chinese culture and classic provokes severe criticism.

Rey Chow sharply points out in the introduction of her book *Writing Diaspora: Tactics of Intervention in Contemporary Cultural Studies* that Owen's claim is of racial discrimination and is more self-concerned than academically oriented:

> This is the anxiety that the Chinese past which he has undertaken to penetrate is evaporating and that the sinologist himself is the abandoned subject ... writers of the "third world" like Bei Dao now appear not as the oppressed but as oppressors, who aggress against the "first world" sinologist by robbing him of his love ... Owen's real complaint is that he is the victim of a monstrous world order in front of which a sulking impotence like his is the only claim to truth. (Chow 4)

Zhang Longxi, in the article "Out of the Cultural Ghetto" in his book *Mighty Opposites: From Dichotomies to Differences in the Comparative Study of China*, furthers this criticism to a disciplinary and cultural level. Owen's disapproval of Chinese modern poetry not only indicates his personal unwillingness to step out of his intellectual comfort zone of the classical Chinese poetry but also impedes disciplinary and cultural development. Barriers are established between disciplines, and Chinese literature and culture are trapped within a ghetto. Owen's idea, as Zhang suggests, is not an expression of personal preferences; rather, he makes biased dichotomies between China and the West, national and international, and the classical and modern:

> It would indeed be fortunate if a scholar of the classical Chinese literature were willing to step into the area of modern studies, for the willingness to pull down the usual barriers between fields of scholarly pursuit is a prerequisite for success in the attempt to get out of the cultural ghetto ... his [Owen's] views tend to ghettoize Chinese literature and to define China and the West, "national" and "international" poetry, "as mutually exclusive, as closures." (Zhang Longxi, *Mighty Opposites* 133)

Owen's readiness to establish dichotomies between China and the West, national and international, and the classical and modern derives from "his predilection for cultural differences" and his insistence about the assumed "incommensurability" between the different ways to understand poetry in China and the West (Ibid.). Owen's presumption about Chinese poetry, as

Zhang summarizes, is that it "remains in a fundamental continuum with history actuality"; however, "Western poetry is fictional and detached from history" (Ibid. 134), and "the intertwining of poetry with history" is adopted by Owen "as the most important criterion to disqualify Bei Dao's work" (Ibid. 133). By emphasizing the differences, Owen isolates and ghettoizes Chinese literature and culture. It seems to Owen that any poems created without associating with Chinese history, the classic, and tradition should not be called "Chinese literature" but rather "literature that began in Chinese language" (Ibid. 131).

Owen's claim reminds us of Hulme's obsession with the postcolonial reading of *The Tempest*. Hulme's familiarity with postcolonial studies determines his preference and faith in applying his specialized knowledge to interpreting the play *The Tempest*. The historical connection of the postcolonial reading is the evidence held by him to validate his perspective and at the same time evaluate and exclude other possible perspectives. In this way, not only do postcolonial studies remain a closed field without addressing the external but relevant fields of studies, but *The Tempest* has also been labeled as a work reserved for postcolonial studies, ghettoized and isolated within that closed field. Unlike Owen, whose resistance against the newly emerging "world poetry" originates from his nostalgia for the classical Chinese literature, Hulme not only competes with new branches of criticism about *The Tempest* but also refutes the traditional reading of the play. Vickers's defense of *The Tempest*, for example, refers to a less politically oriented but more humanity-related and more abstract argument that "the dichotomy of art and nature was important in Renaissance thought and in Shakespeare" (Vickers 416). Hulme, however, sarcastically points out that Vickers holds the argument as "a simple truth" (Hulme). It seems that *The Tempest* in Hulme's mind is not only confined to the closed field of postcolonial studies but also remains stagnant over the single moment of creation along the historical continuum.

What, then, is a better way to read the classic play in this age of world literature? Zhang's idea about the multiple perspectives of Chinese studies in his article "The True Face of Mount Lu: On the Significance of Perspectives and Paradigms" can certainly shed light on this question. Like Eliot, who argues for the inexhaustible diversity embedded within a classic work, Zhang suggests that Chinese studies are to be illuminated with multiple perspectives rather than relying on a sole angle. Zhang initiates his argument by quoting a classical Chinese poem:

> Viewed horizontally a range; a cliff from the side,
> It differs as we move high or low, or far or nearby.
> We do not know the true face of Mount Lu,
> Because we are all ourselves inside.
> — Su Shi, "Written on the Wall of the Temple of West Woods." (qtd. in Zhang Longxi, "The True Face of Mount Lu" 58)

Mount Lu reflects itself into different shapes that are subjected to the diverse perspectives of the viewers. No single angle can afford to depict and determine the whole picture of Mount Lu. Like Mount Lu, Chinese studies draw and deserve multiple perspectives. Neither Chinese people, who are regarded as insiders with the advantage of familiarity with the local culture, nor sinologists, who are considered outsiders with the benefit of an objective perspective, can claim superiority or singularity in Chinese studies. It "requires integration of different views from different perspectives" (Ibid. 68). "But such integration," as Zhang proceeds with his argument, "is not a simple juxtaposition of insiders' and outsiders' views; it is more of an act of interaction and mutual illumination than adding up native Chinese scholarship and Western Sinology" (Ibid.).

When rebutting Owen's claim about Bei Dao, David Damrosch expresses resonating opinions in his article "World Literature, National Contexts." Damrosch points out that "rather than being a rootless cosmopolitan, Bei Dao is doubly or multiply linked to events and audiences at home and abroad" (Damrosch, "World Literature, National Contexts" 527). Bei Dao's poetry not only relates to the domestic environment of China, where his "prosody may be subverting Maoist calls to abandon the complexities of aristocratic poetry and return to the purity of the old *Shih Ching* (*Book of Songs*)," but also responds to external impact, such as the "translations of earlier Spanish-language poets like Rubén Darío and Federico García Lorca" (Ibid. 526). It seems that in this age of world literature, a solid mastery of national and special knowledge is not sufficient to sustain the dynamic development of world literature, but scholars today need to adopt a more "general" and macro perspective and be aware of and alert to the changes beyond national and disciplinary borders. The relationship between "generalist" and "specialist" is mutually indispensable and reciprocal. Compared to the "generalist," the specialist "is not always in the best position to assess the dramatically different terms on which a work may engage with a distant culture" (Ibid. 517). At the same time, a "specialist's knowledge is the major safeguard against the generalist's own will to power over texts that otherwise all too easily become grist for the mill of a preformed historical argument or theoretical system" (Ibid.). It is only when they work in collaboration that we can "understand they work effectively in its new cultural or theoretical context while at the same time getting it right in a fundamental way with reference to the source culture" (Ibid.).

Eliot's idea about the classic, Zhang's opinion about perspectives, and Damrosch's argument about collaboration between the generalist and specialist ground our rebuttal against Hulme's defense of the postcolonial reading as the only validated approach to *The Tempest*. The postcolonial reading cannot exhaust the classic play, which, as Eliot suggests, reflects "variety," "completeness," and "relatedness." We cannot grasp the whole picture of the play by adhering to a single perspective, and the overemphasis on the special knowledge makes scholars less alert to the external and emerging changes. Possible connection and potential communication with these new changes are dispelled, and the classic play is ghettoized and forgotten. Hulme's insistence about the play's historical connection is certainly justified and counts as serious scholarship, but to deliberately disregard other worthwhile perspectives and downplay the importance of communication and illumination between different angles should be avoided in this age of world literature.

William Hamlin, one of the scholars whom Hulme criticizes in his article "Stormy Weather: Misreading the Postcolonial Tempest," seems to provide a more open-minded approach to studying the play. Hamlin suggests "shifting the contextual ground from the highly politicized discourse of colonialism to the more taxonomic, speculative, polyvalent, and autonomous discourse of ethnography" (qtd. in Hulme). By doing so, Hamlin intends to show that "one may retain the New World context and the historicist approach without necessarily committing oneself to the near dogmatism that seems endemic to colonialist readings" (Ibid.). Hulme ironically describes Hamlin's attempt as "in best pluralist fashion" (Hulme). Hulme again declares his rigid commitment to the postcolonial reading of *The Tempest* and is reluctant to associate it with other perspectives, just as Damrosch states in his article "World Literature, National Contexts" that "the more committed today's Shakespeareans become to understanding literature within a cultural context, the less likely they are to feel comfortable in comparing Shakespeare and Kalidasa" (Damrosch, "World Literature, National Contexts" 515). Hamlin's proposal reflects and respects the diversity embedded in the classic and acknowledges the value of the contribution made by different perspectives. Instead of denying and displacing a postcolonial reading of the classic play, Hamlin supplements and supports the perspective by introducing and relating to other perspectives. It is not a simple integration of perspectives or the coexistence of "plural" interpretations, but different perspectives are taken together to illuminate and benefit one another mutually.

Hamlin's idea reminds us of Damrosch's strategy to combine "hypercanon" and "countercanon" in world literature studies. The classic works that are dominant and popular may impede the entry of less familiar works into the list of canons and threaten the circulation and readership of these less accessed works. This situation should be improved, especially in this age of world literature, where communication between literatures needs most urgently to break through the closed circle of "canons." Damrosch in his article "World Literature in a Postcolonial, Hypercanonical Age" suggests combining "hypercanon" and "countercanon" in world literature studies. To completely overthrow the "hypercanons" seems unfeasible and unnecessary, and to recklessly deny the value of the classic and traditions also counts as a provincial and parochial gesture. Instead, we can associate the two kinds of canons with each other by establishing a reciprocal relationship between them: As Damrosch proposes, "we should resist the hegemony of the hypercanon, yet as long as it's a fact of life, we should also turn it into our advantage" (Damrosch, "World Literature in a Postcolonial, Hypercanonical Age" 50). We could use the widely acknowledged classics to smooth the way for less known "countercanons" and to link and relate the former to less popular literary classics that are from different cultures and that domestic readers may not have been familiarized with. In this way, not only does the value of less familiar classics gain more acknowledgment from expanded geographical areas and academic fields, but the traditional classics can also benefit from this kind of communication. For example, new and inspirational interpretations can be explored and derived, and stereotyped interpretations of the classic can be corrected and refined.

To boost communication and diversity, however, is not an excuse to tolerate any perspectives and interpretations, some of which are irresponsibly formulated. In fact, Hulme's concern about "pluralist fashion" and "coexistence" is not completely unreasonable. To ghettoize a piece of the classic or a certain culture is rightly criticized, but to twist the classic works and cultural traditions and detach them completely from their origins to fit in with the predetermined assumptions of a different culture would seem to be another kind of ghettoization. China and Chinese literature studies, as discussed above, not only underwent the threat of ghettoization but also experienced the danger caused by another extreme, which Damrosch phrases "an absolute disconnect from its culture of origin" (Damrosch, "World Literature, National Contexts" 521). Translation is a form of communication between classics from different cultures. It wipes out the linguistic barriers and expands the readership of the classic from less familiar cultures. Yet whether translations can faithfully transmit the information and feelings in the original classics becomes a main concern. Sometimes "creativity" dominates the translation process and betrays the classic in an unreasonable way.

Ezra Pound's translation and "invention" about Chinese poetry can be an example. Pound suggests that "Chinese poetry, written in ideograms that he believed to be 'shorthand pictures of actions and processes,' explores the pictorial values of the characters to the utmost" (Zhang Longxi, "The 'Tao' and the 'Logos'" 385). These characters do not become the outcomes of abstract thinking but only stiff imitations of material things in the natural world. The character "習" exampled in the article has been split into two parts: the upper part, "羽," (feather) and the lower part, "白," (white). The original meaning of the character denoting *learning* has thus been transformed into a picture of a "white feature" (Ibid. 389). Unlike languages such as English, which are formulated to follow phonetic rules, the Chinese language and thinking system seem to be visually oriented. This bizarre assumption about Chinese literary classics was inaccurately taken as a breakthrough of the "logos" thinking system, which is advocated by Jacque Derrida and widely accepted within Western culture. Chinese classic poetry in Pound's translation was twisted and lost. Hulme's rebuttal against the "pluralist fashion" in studying *The Tempest* is grounded on the claim that alternative readings of *The Tempest* that attempt to parallel the postcolonial interpretation contain "misreading" and "error" (Hulme). To Hulme, alternatives are invalid; however, here, as we can see, it is precisely the attempt to ghettoize Chinese culture and literature that creates a fallacy. To respect and refer to the original work and cultural backgrounds faithfully and seriously is a rewarding act that should be appreciated and advocated, just as Damrosch suggests when he illuminates how specialists' knowledge assists generalists in "getting it right in a fundamental way with reference to the source culture" in world literature studies (Damrosch, "World Literature in a Postcolonial, Hypercanonical Age" 517).

To reduce and restrict a piece of the classic to something that only deserves a single interpretation and to prioritize one particular perspective for perceiving a culture is questionable. Thanks to the renaissance of the concept of world literature, recent years have witnessed the prosperity of cultural diversity and lively communications. Making the classic and cultures ghettoized like isolated and scattered islands is not feasible when bridges and tunnels are built and found in between. We expect and welcome a new *A Tempest,* which will reveal and emphasize another inspiring aspect of the classic play *The Tempest,* and we anticipate and applaud contributions from a new perspective to the whole picture or the "true face" of China studies and Chinese literature and culture. At the same time, diversity and multiplicity do not wipe out affinities within different classics and cultures. Differences deliberately fabricated should not overwhelm the affinities that enable the communication between literatures and cultures. We reach through the tunnel to relate and recognize the affinities, and we overcome the tunnel vision to realize and respect the differences.

Chapter Five

Footnotes Where the Classic and Creativity Interact

5.1 How the Classic and Creativity Interact in Footnotes

The classic and creativity interact in footnotes. Footnotes can either be the interpretive ones that are given by scholars or commentators other than the authors or the informative ones that are given by the authors themselves in their own pieces of work so as to supply readers with supplementary or supportive materials. In the first kind of footnotes, scholars comment on the classics with subjective and expressive opinions or interpret the classics with creative and adaptive perspectives. Such footnotes enable the individual and the creative to be incorporated within the classics. Personal insights and impressions are introduced into this kind of interaction with the classics. In world literature, the interaction between the classic and creativity in such footnotes becomes more complicated and yet more vigorous. Interpretive footnotes attached to a piece of the classic may constitute voices from people from different cultural backgrounds. Their distinctive personal preferences and various fields of special knowledge can result in different ways of communicating with the classic. Before world literature, the interaction between the classic and creativity in footnotes could transcend time and could be taken away from the historical continuum; for example, footnotes that reflected the originality of different times could extend the life of the classic and adapt the classic within new eras or new contexts by introducing new perspectives and interpretations into the classic. In world literature, footnotes also expand the geographical areas and disciplinary fields where the classic is well received and researched by individual and creative talents. Footnotes that contain creative interpretations and localizations from diverse cultural backgrounds contribute to the study and circulation of the classic beyond national and cultural borders.

Footnotes that are given by authors themselves in their own pieces of work also witness this encounter between creativity and the counterparts of the classic. To supplement their arguments, authors quote and refer to the classic in footnotes. They relate to and communicate with precedent works. They make connections between their own thoughts and the insights of their predecessors. Moreover, from the carefully selected quotations of the classic, the subjectively formulated connections between the quotations, the individual attitudes conveyed through the comparison of quotations, and the personal communications with precedent scholars and masters, we can detect authors' creativity embedded within the footnotes. Authors are also entitled to shift their perspective and adopt a different narrative in footnotes. In the footnotes, they can become comentators who criticize the classics mentioned in the text. They may resemble readers expressing emotional feelings about the quoted classics. They can even imitate designers tailoring footnotes into a personal style to accomplish a particular purpose. For example, references that are as lengthy as the texts and footnotes that are deliberately designed as part of the dramatic plot certainly reflect authors' personal intentions.

Compared with footnotes that are provided by scholars and commentators, footnotes that are provided by the authors themselves witness more complex and yet intriguing interactions between the classic and creativity in this age of world literature. Footnotes, within which first-hand references to the classics from different cultures are given and secondary commentaries about different cultural classic works are quoted, are proof of an author's competence in adopting a complete and comparative perspective in world literature studies. To arrange and approach these quotations in the footnotes according to the author's own preferences or personal perspectives, however, may provoke fierce discussion and strong feelings. For example, making the information about the classics from different and other cultures and literatures "sheltered" in footnotes would seem to jeopardize the impartiality that scholars make an effort to construct in their creatively and unprecedentedly made comparisons or summations of world literatures. Opposing voices can be easily ignited when questions about the struggle and communication between "centered" and "periphery" cultures are heatedly discussed in this age of world literature.

Footnotes in translations also reflect the complicated relationship and interactions between the classic and creativity, especially in this age of world literature. Translation makes the communication between different cultures possible and prosperous. Yet readers may need necessary contextual information to facilitate their full understanding of a piece of translation, and it is always the footnotes that they turn to for knowledge about "other cultures" in translations. The problem, however, is whether the translation should be faithfully consistent with the original classic or whether it should creatively adapt and assimilate the classic for the target context. The struggle or wrestle between the classic from their cultural origins and the creativity and demands of the target cultures becomes appealing to scholars of world literature studies.

5.2   The Importance of Footnotes and the Paradoxical Features of Footnotes

When A. N. Whitehead try to argue for the supreme significance of Plato, he makes a celebrated remark that "the safest general characterization of the European philosophical tradition is that it consists of a series of footnotes to Plato" (Whitehead 39). To Whitehead, "the European philosophical tradition," like footnotes, is derivative and subordinate when it is compared to Plato's ideas, which are original and primary. By reducing "the European philosophical tradition" to "a series of footnotes," Whitehead makes his point. Distinct from the "body" of the text, footnotes indeed seem to be secondary.

Such a conventional impression of footnotes, however, is not always true. Before the recent renaissance of the concept of world literature, footnotes had already been more than supplements. They are targets for study that are no less worthy than the texts. Footnotes, if arranged in a careful design, can also be the medium through which important ideas are conveyed and substantiated. The lengthy footnotes appended to the poem *The Waste Land,* for example, can hardly be overlooked and draw no less attention than the poem itself. In addition, the dense allusions and traditions contained in these footnotes deserve and provoke as much serious thinking as the poem itself does. The footnotes in *The Waste Land* reflect and help to realize Eliot's idea of how to relate to the classic and tradition in individual writing. They even convey messages that serve as criticism and interpretation of the poem. Footnotes are also important in ancient Chinese literary works. In *The Book of Poetry*, it was literary critics and specialists other than the authors who provided the notes. Most of the notes are subjective understandings and research findings instead of objective information. These notes not only facilitate readers' understanding of the archaic poems but also associate the poems with their contemporary ideologies so as to preserve the book and ensure it is handed down to further generations.

In this age of world literature, footnotes become more significant in the sense that the study of footnotes entails two questions that are heatedly discussed today: What is the relationship between national literature and world literature, and how can you balance the original culture and the target culture in translation? In Franco Moretti's "Conjectures on World Literature," which features "distant reading" and unexpectedly large "chunks" of footnotes, references to national literature that are supposed to constitute material evidence to support his argument appear in the footnotes instead. Such a gesture of placing national literature in footnotes as secondary information while emphasizing ideas of universality and generality about world literature in the text shows exactly how "distant reading" works. Footnotes therefore participate in Moretti's experiment with the idea of "distant reading" in the same article where the method is proposed. The use of footnotes in translations has also become an intriguing question today. In "World Literature, National Contexts," David Damrosch discusses how the length of footnotes affects the readership of the translations of *The Tale of Genji*. Translators can therefore no longer underestimate the importance of footnotes when it comes to the circulation and reception of translations. Footnotes are no longer merely footnotes.

In terms of content, references are to be found in footnotes. They contain extra and derivative information that supplements the "body" of the text. They are not supposed to satisfy readers' cravings for ingenious insights, and they do not expect as much scrutiny as the text does. If given too frequently with too many unfamiliar messages, footnotes can even confuse and frustrate readers. Giving footnotes in that case would seem to be more of a way for authors to construct authority as academic professionals and to impress readers with their erudition. Appeals to abandon scholarly notes have long been voiced. An article that appeared in *New York Times* on August 14, 1996, entitled "Scholars Desert an Old Tradition in a Search for Wider Appeal," argues that "scholarly citation, as they had come to believe, was one of the building blocks of civilization" (Honan). This idea is further supported by the quoted words from then managing director of Harvard University Press, who said, "And our marketing department tells us that footnotes scare people off" (Ibid.).

At the same time, the importance of footnotes as a sign of conscientious scholarship is recognized and defended by some scholars. In their article "The Footnote, in Theory," Anne H. Stevens and Jay Williams argue that "a fundamental function of the humanities footnote" is that "it allows us a means of evaluating the level of scholarship of an essay," and they observe that "today, footnotes in a scholarly essay are not uniformly marginal, minor, or digressive" (Stevens and Williams 211). Anthony Grafton is the individual to whom they attribute these ideas. His book *The Footnote: A Curious History* is considered an indispensable resource for footnote studies. To Grafton, footnotes not only prove but also persuade (Grafton, *The Footnote* 22). Stevens and Williams summarize his ideas and suggest that "we look to them [footnotes] for proof that the author has sufficiently covered the field, that enough evidence has been marshaled, that the status of the evidence has been sufficiently questioned" (Stevens and Williams 211). Footnotes persuade readers that authors are being responsible and critical but not necessarily pedantic.

In fact, the reliability of those subjective attitudes indicated through footnotes is likely to be questioned. When Anthony Grafton explains how footnotes perform an act of persuasion on readers, he refers to the inevitable subjectivity embedded in them:

> In practice, moreover, every annotator rearranges materials to prove a point, interprets them in an individual way, and omits those that do not meet a necessarily personal standard of relevance. The very next person to pass through the same archival materials will probably line them up and sort them out quite differently. (Grafton, "The Footnote from De Thou to Ranke" 56).

The "individual" and "personal" choices and arrangements of references in the footnotes, which suggest and support individual opinions and feelings, may not be considered as responsible or critical as intended; rather, they may be regarded as unconvincing and inconsistent. In his essay "Marginalia," Edgar Allen Poe states that "it may be as well to observe, however, that just as the goodness of your true pun is in the direct ratio of its intolerability, so is nonsense the essential sense of the Marginal Note" (Poe 177). It seems reasonable for Poe as a romanticist to emphasize "a spontaneous overflow of powerful feelings" (Coleridge and Wordsworth 183), but footnotes within which personal feelings are revealed can sometimes become targets of criticism. They can be viewed as idiosyncratic prejudices or biased interpretations that are to be justifiably ignored or minimized.

To some scholars, however, giving footnotes that are expressive of strong attitudes and emotions is an academic act that should rightly be advocated. In "The Footnote, in Theory," Stevens and Williams say that they seem to have proposed a "risky venture" (Stevens and Williams 210). They try to discover and define the identity of theory and the journal *Critical Inquiry* by investigating the footnotes appended to the essays in the journal. "Polemical" and "passionate," as they point out, are the two most endorsed labels of *Critical Inquiry*. The more polemical and passionate the essay, the more likely it is that strong thoughts and feelings will be provoked and expressed (Ibid.). Footnotes, by which the "critical responses and rejoinders" are accompanied and to which "the feelings of anger, disgust, and [betrayal]" are attached, enable dialogues between essays and authors (Ibid.). As Shari Benstock suggests in her article "At the Margin of Discourse: Footnotes in the Fictional Text," footnotes can be "addressing a larger, extratextual world in an effort to relate this text to other texts, to negotiate the middle ground between this author and other authors," and "the critical stance" can be shifted in footnotes, which "becomes self-conscious, argumentative, defensive, even quarrelsome, or perhaps playful, ingenuous, or ironic" (Benstock 204). In this way, footnotes are incorporated into the text to perform the function of stimulating and facilitating the (emotional) exchange of ideas within an essay, thus making the essay polemical and passionate.

5.3 Footnotes in *The Waste Land*: References to the Past

The paradoxical features of footnotes had already manifested themselves before the renaissance of world literature today. *The Waste Land* is said to be incoherent and inconsistent, and, interestingly, these have become the most intriguing and the most discussed aspects of the poem. The five parts of the poem are so different from each other in "style and situation" that they constitute "a framework within which many complex themes and moods interact" more than a poem (Gish 29); however, aside from the "complex themes and moods" expressed in the texts of the poem, the long and complicated footnotes are also responsible for the poem's lack of unity.

The Waste Land is a highly allusive poem. Allusions appear frequently in the poem. Footnotes have to be provided either to remind readers of the works that are alluded to or to explain to readers how the allusions are made. To grasp the full meaning of the poem, readers have to constantly turn to the footnotes while they are in the middle of reading. This would definitely make the reading process fragmented and interrupted. Just as Nancy Gish suggests, footnotes have "the effect of directing the reader's attention away from the immediate experience of the poem" (Ibid.). Because of the footnotes, we cannot read the poem smoothly and can therefore hardly consider the poem coherent and unified. The content in the footnotes also distracts readers from the poem. Literary works such as the *Inferno* by Dante, *Metamorphoses* by Ovid, and *Confessions* by Augustine are alluded to in the poem, and references to them appear in the footnotes. To most readers, these are heavy works and can be unfamiliar and complicated. Readers can hardly expect to understand the allusions in an instant with a glimpse at the footnotes. They have to step out of the discourse of the poem and ponder over the works to which the footnotes allude; therefore, the footnotes not only distort the text of the poem but also disrupt the direct encounter between the reader and the poem. Such intertextuality detaches readers not only from the poem but also from their own time. Most of the literary works that are alluded to are classics, and their appearance in the footnotes of the poem blurs time. The past has transcended to the present, while the present is traced back to the past. The juxtaposition of different literary works and the confusion in time contribute to the incoherence of the poem; however, instead of disadvantaging the poem, the incoherence and inconsistency of the poem distinguish it from others. Footnotes are applied to support and enhance this distinctiveness of the poem.

When T. S. Eliot explains why he appended the footnotes to the poem *The Waste Land*, he begins with an exclamation, "The notes to *The Waste Land*!"; this is to express his surprise at the unexpected importance that has been attached to the footnotes by critics and readers (Eliot, *The Waste Land* 108). The original intention, as Eliot playfully indicates, was to expand the "inconveniently short" poem and "bulk out the volume" of it as an independent book (Ibid.). In addition, as Eliot proceeds, "they can never be unstuck," as it would affect the readership of the poem. Readers at that time would not buy editions that excluded the footnotes (Ibid.). In the following, however, I would argue that to add footnotes to the poem is by no means for the convenience of publication, nor is it a strategy for promotion; rather, the footnotes not only support Eliot's argument about how to adapt tradition to the new but also perform a critical and interpretive act on the poem.

126 As Eliot himself says, the footnotes shield him from critics' fierce accusations of plagiarism (Ibid.). *The Waste Land* is a highly allusive poem. Images and fragments from previous works seem to be pieced together in the poem. Footnotes that explicitly give references to these images and fragments appear to show a more serious academic attitude and will hopefully cushion the blow of the criticism. Quite opposite to this expectation, however, the footnotes have been criticized as "the remarkable exposition of bogus scholarship" (Ibid.). This would seem to be an unreasonable censure, but reviewing the poem and the long footnotes, we can indeed find that some of the footnotes appear sloppy and even defiant, such as the footnote to line 199, "I do not know the origin of the ballad from which these lines are taken: it was reported to me from Sydney, Australia" (Ibid. 72); the footnote to line 221, "This may not appear as exact as Sappho's lines, but I have in mind the 'long shore' or 'dory' fisherman, who returns at nightfall" (Ibid. 73); and the footnote to line 360, "The following lines were stimulated by the account of one of the Antarctic expeditions (I forget which, but I think one of Shackleton's): it was related that the party of explorers, at the extremity of their strength, had the constant delusion" (Ibid. 74).

Unlike the other footnotes, which have specific and adequate information about the works to which they refer, these three footnotes are replete with obscurity and uncertainty. The word *I* creates a sense of subjectivity. It seems that Eliot deliberately emphasizes his authorship of the poem in the footnotes, but the footnotes do not sound objective and thus lack authority. And terms such as *do not know* and *forget* may be deemed unacceptable by some serious scholars and critics. The seeming sloppiness of these footnotes, however, does not result from the indiscreet academic attitudes of the author; rather, it shows how Eliot adapts the tradition to the new. In his introduction to *The Waste Land and Other Poems*, Frank Kermode quotes lines from Eliot's poem "Little Gidding" to illustrate how the style of the poem "permitted a view of history as without perspective, and a mode of composition that did not forget the past but perceived its methods as effects of mere custom rather than law" (Ibid. xxi). The quoted lines from the poem are as follows:

Last year's fruit is eaten,
And the fulfilled beast shall kick the empty pail.
For the last year's words belong to last year's language
And next year's words await another voice. (Ibid.)

To Eliot, to adapt literary tradition is not to rigidly adhere to the original words of it, nor should the tradition be implemented as law, which may limit and impede the new. Tradition is not mandatory but customary. It has a profound impact on the new in the sense that traces of it are embedded in the minds of writers of later generations. They are easily remembered and readily quoted in new works, and, more importantly, they are adapted by and for "another voice." To return to the exampled notes, in the note to line 221, the "long shore" and the "dory" fisherman "who returns at nightfall" are both imageries that Eliot borrows from Sappho's poems. These imageries suit the new poem that Eliot creates. The elements selected from the ancient poems serve as proper material for constructing an image of the sailor's homecoming. References to the classics are naturally and reasonably embedded in Eliot's new poem. In fact, relating to the classics naturally and creatively is much better than consciously and rigidly quoting these works word for word. Eliot must have these classics stored in his mind and let them flow out spontaneously when he writes. Whether he remembers and presents the exact words of the original works in his poem seems to be an issue that does not merit distracting the reader from the fluency and consistency of his work.

In fact, the other notes to the poem, which sound more serious and formal than these three ones, may also become the targets of criticism for their "bogus scholarship." They are informative, detailed, and accurate, citing the names of the works, the authors, and the page numbers. Some notes, such as the note to lines 60 and 63, even include quotations in the original and foreign languages:

60. Cf. Baudelaire:
"Fourmillante cité, cité pleine de rèves,
   Où le spectre en plein jour raccroche le passant."

63. Cf. Inferno, III. 55–57:

> "Si lunga tratta
> di gente, ch'io non avrei mai creduto
> che morte tanta n'avesse disfatta." (Ibid. 71)

Informative and detailed as they are, however, most of the notes are merely quotations without further elaboration either about the original works or about their importance to the poem. Readers may not be as knowledgeable and multilingual as they are assumed to be. Unlike Eliot himself and the targeted critics of the notes, they may not be able to recall or understand all the referenced works with a mere glimpse. To readers, these notes may not communicate the meaning of the poem but instead might complicate the poem. The notes may not facilitate their understanding but become an extra burden. Therefore, the notes seem to be intended more to impress the readers with the shocking erudition of the author than to impart knowledge to the readers, hence the "bogus scholarship."

The footnotes in *The Waste Land,* however, are not limited to facts or numbers only. They can also fulfill the useful function of criticizing and interpreting the poem. They not only contain criticism of the quoted classics but also act as criticism of the poem. For example, the note to line 218 is as follows:

> 218. Tiresias, although a mere spectator and not indeed a "character," is yet the most important personage in the poem, uniting all the rest. Just as the one-eyed merchant, seller of currants, melts into the Phoenician Sailor, and the latter is not wholly distinct from Ferdinand Prince of Naples, so all the women are one woman, and the two sexes meet in Tiresias. What Tiresias sees, in fact, is the substance of the poem. The whole passage from Ovid is of great anthropological interest ... (Ibid. 72–73)

Following the above part, Eliot quotes the original passage in Latin from Ovid's *Metamorphoses*. As Kermode summarizes in his explanatory notes, it deals with "the sex change of Tiresias" (Ibid. 103). Unlike the other notes, where the author's subjective opinions are rare or absent, this note begins with Eliot's own observations and comments on Tiresias. Eliot characterizes Tiresias as a "spectator" and points out that its function is "uniting all the rest." The voice is personal and strong as Eliot uses superlatives to describe the importance he bestows upon the role. A comparison with the Phoenician sailor, who is also a character in the poem, is consciously made to prove and illustrate why Tiresias is special: Two perspectives (two sexes) are mixed in him. Most importantly, Eliot proceeds to reach an illuminating conclusion that Tiresias not only unites the poem but also serves as the narrator, as "what he sees" is "the substance of the poem" (Ibid. 73). Sharing this idea in the footnotes not only enlightens the readers and facilitates their understanding of the allusion but also provides critics with firm evidence on which further analysis of the poem can be grounded. Frank Kermode, for example, based on this note, takes a step further in saying that "Tiresias is the point of view from which the exemplars of wasteland degeneracy are seen to meet" (Ibid. 103). An important message can be derived from Eliot's and Kermode's notes: that Eliot, like Tiresias, is both the narrator and the spectator of the poem. Two perspectives are mixed in Eliot: one as the author of the poem and the other as the critic. The footnotes enable Eliot to transition between the two different roles, just like Tiresias. The notes are therefore not all cold facts about the tradition but include instructive thoughts that inspire us to further explore the poem. They are important to the poem, and they are not "bogus scholarship," as has been alleged.

5.4 Footnotes in *The Book of Poetry*: Subjective Interpretation of the Classic

Unlike in *The Waste Land*, footnotes in ancient Chinese literature are not provided at the bottom of the pages, nor are they separated from the texts. As the texts are typeset vertically in ancient Chinese literature, footnotes are given directly underneath the words to which they are attached. They are interlineal notes and commentaries rather than footnotes as such. Although they distinguish themselves with smaller fonts, in ancient Chinese literature, it is not unusual to see that notes and commentaries occupy most of the space on a page, with only several words of the texts scattered between them. Readers can hardly overlook them when they read along the lines, as the notes and commentaries are so densely merged with the texts.

Another difference is that footnotes in ancient Chinese literature are provided by commentators instead of by the writers. The footnotes can be records of their personal opinions and understandings. Some may include extra knowledge that the commentators found helpful and relevant. The subjectivity of the footnotes, however, does not make it less rewarding to take them seriously in ancient Chinese literature studies. Their impact is not to be disregarded in the sense that these footnotes not only enable readers of later generations to understand the ancient and obscure texts but also provide them with new approaches to interpreting the texts. The footnotes contextualize the texts in different periods, reflecting different ideological emphases.

Taking the footnotes in *The Book of Poetry* as an example, giving footnotes to *The Book of Poetry* is a scholarly activity that has persisted for a long time. It can be traced back to as early as Confucius's time (Xia 4). Hundreds of scholars have made lifelong and painstaking efforts to interpret the poems and record their findings in "zhu shu," which means notes that help to explain the meanings of the texts (Ibid.). The reason why the footnotes are essential to *The Book of Poetry* lies in the fact that they have facilitated people's understanding of the archaic poems. Without these footnotes, the ancient and obscure poems would be destined to become obsolete and forgotten. *The Book of Poetry* was compiled with poems that were created or performed by people living in the pre-Qin era, which is over two thousand years ago. Since then, the words, the grammatical structure, and the phonetics of daily language have undergone such constant and dramatic changes that the poems already sounded archaic in the Han dynasty (a dynasty that emerged shortly after the Qin dynasty) (Ibid.). The meanings of these poems were also consciously sacrificed due to the special rhythmical and formal limitations of poetry at that time (Ibid.). All these factors result in severe difficulty in understanding the poems in *The Book of Poetry*.

To understand the archaic poems, readers must depend on the footnotes.

Although the footnotes given and revised by different schools and generations may sometimes be criticized as prejudiced and inadequate and different footnotes may even contradict one another, they are still indispensable for these poems. Without them, the poems in *The Book of Poetry* would have appeared as a "pile of ancient characters that are incomprehensible" (Ibid. 5), and they could have easily been forgotten. The footnotes guarantee and extend the comprehensibility of *The Book of Poetry;* thanks to the footnotes, readers of the contemporary time (which is so far away from the time of pre-Qin) not only have access to the archaic texts but also have the capability to read and appreciate these literary masterpieces.

Not only have these footnotes communicated the meanings of the ancient poems to readers, but they have also recreated and refined the meanings of the poems so as to make them fit in better with the new ideologies that have emerged in new eras. In fact, footnotes in ancient Chinese literature are similar to literary criticism. Both are given by commentators instead of authors, and both concern subjective opinions. Both are supposed to be secondary to the original, and yet both are more essential than they are assumed to be. Oscar Wilde suggests that criticism requires more creativity than does art and that it "treats the work of art simply as a starting point for a new creation" (Wilde, *Oscar Wilde* 263). It is legitimate to say that literary criticism is not subordinate to the original but superior to the original. We may not agree with the claim that criticism necessarily surpasses the original, but the gesture to attach significance to criticism is to be appreciated. Criticism gives new life to the original works.

Interestingly, the footnotes in *The Book of Poetry* have similar functions. No matter how archaic the poems sound, footnotes can always renew them and facilitate their adaptation to the new ideologies that emerge in new eras. For example, in the Han Dynasty, the ruling class, to consolidate their sovereignty, established a system of thought that grounded the claim that the power of the emperor was bestowed by the divine and the immortal (Xia 67); it should not and could not be overthrown. *The Book of Poetry,* conversely, contains many poems that address earthly issues such as love, nature, and labor, and these poems were not sacred prophecies of the divine but folk songs sung by commoners. Therefore, to bridge the gap between the book and the ideology of that time, scholars created footnotes that excessively emphasize the divine and mysterious aspects of the poems (Ibid. 68). Thanks to these footnotes, *The Book of Poetry* was given new life and survived the supreme power.

Such over-interpretation and deliberate misunderstanding of the poems, however, certainly provoked fierce reactions. Criticism and different opinions were voiced against these footnotes. Some scholars in the Han Dynasty argued that to provide footnotes that unreasonably emphasized the mysterious aspects of the poems was to transgress the bounds of decency because Confucius says that a decent man should not talk about the mystery (Ibid.). Scholars of later times, conversely, were opposed to political interference in giving footnotes. Some of them treated the poems as pieces of great literature and gave aesthetic evaluations in their footnotes; others chose to focus on the historical value of the poems and provided a contextual analysis of the poems in their footnotes (Ibid. 6).

As we can see now, however, the study of *The Book of Poetry* has not become less productive because of the ongoing "internal conflicts." On the contrary, the varied and competing footnotes contribute new insight and give new life to *The Book of Poetry*. The study of the footnotes of *The Book of Poetry* has become so prosperous that it is established as an independent and specialized field of study in which different footnotes to *The Book of Poetry* are historically situated, specifically introduced, and critically compared. In addition, because of the footnotes, *The Book of Poetry* becomes a piece of the classic that is inexhaustible and that has drawn constant attention throughout the history of Chinese literature studies.

Let us now look at some specific poems in *The Book of Poetry*. The first poem in *The Book of Poetry*, "关雎," which is translated as "Cooing and Wooing," may be the most familiar piece to readers (Xu 2). The translations of the first four lines of the poem are as follows:

By riverside a pair,
Of turtle doves are cooing

There is a maiden fair,
Whom a young man is wooing. (Ibid.)

These lines are not only known to the majority of readers but can even be recited by toddlers. The short lines rhyme in Chinese, which makes them easy to remember. The meaning of the lines in Chinese, however, is not as obvious or literal as it seems to be. The lines could not be so readily understood or so widely spread if the notes were detached from the poem. The trick lies in the first two Chinese characters, *guan guan*. The meaning of the character *guan* in contemporary Chinese is "close" or "closed," and apparently it can hardly be related or applied to the poem, the context of which deals with love, as we can discern at first glance. In addition, the repetitive use of the character makes it more difficult to force the contemporary meaning of the characters on the poem. To rigidly introduce the contemporary meaning into the poem would result in a bizarre interpretation. Thanks to the note attached, we can solve this problem. The note attached to the lines is given by Mao Heng, a scholar in the Han Dynasty, and the note states that "*guan guan* are harmony sounds of the birds" (Mao et al. 22). In the poem, they are onomatopoeia rather than verbs or adjectives, the function of which they perform in contemporary Chinese. The distinction between the ancient and contemporary meanings of the character is so significant that a wild guess could never help us to decipher the ancient meaning. We need to rely on the footnotes. The footnotes therefore guarantee and extend the comprehensibility of *The Book of Poetry;* thanks to the footnotes, contemporary readers not only have access to the archaic texts but also have the capability to read the poems and appreciate the vividness of the literary masterpieces.

Not only have these footnotes communicated the meanings of the ancient poems to readers, but they have also recreated and refined the meanings of them so as to make the poems fit in better with the ideologies that have emerged or persisted in different eras. Just as we discussed previously, the footnotes in ancient Chinese literature are similar to literary criticism. Both are provided by commentators instead of authors, and both concern subjective opinions. Both are supposed to be secondary to the original, and yet both are more essential than they are assumed to be.

The footnotes in *The Book of Poetry* have similar functions. In particular,

134 the notes to the poem "Jian Jia" fall into this category. The poem's translation in English is as follows:

> Green, green the reed. Frost and dew gleam.
> Where's she I need? Beyond the stream.
> Upstream I go. The way's so long.
> And downstream, lo! She's there among. (Xu 133)

Obviously, this is a love poem, and any further elaborations or explorations are expected to be made out of the topic of love; however, when readers refer to the notes on these lines, they will be surprised to find how such a colloquial and simple poem can be interpreted as an allusion to an ideological and political issue: how to rule the people and the state. Within the notes, we can see the following lines:

> Mao thinks that, although the reed is exuberant, it cannot be used unless the dew on the reed becomes frost, making the reed solid. This is to allude to the fact that, although the state of Qin had a large population, the emperor did not follow the morals to educate the people. Morals that were inherited from the Zhou dynasty were needed to educate the people so that they would follow the emperor and the state would be prosperous and strong ... Going upstream, one cannot reach the destination, as the journey would be long and dangerous. This means that by infringing on the morals, the emperor would distance himself from the right way, and people would not obey. Going downstream, it would be as if one were in the middle of the water. This means that if the emperor rules the people according to the morals, he would be ruling in the right way, and people would follow and obey him willingly. (Mao et al. 240) [1]

Because of the footnotes, this folk poem, which is sung and circulated by common people, unexpectedly becomes a serious allusion. It raises issues about the ideology of the time, which concerns the ruler of the state. In

---

[1] The original is in Chinese. It is translated into English by the author.

this way, the footnotes not only expand the meaning of the poem but also contextualize it within its contemporary ideology. Learning from the failure of the Qin dynasty, the emperors of the Han dynasty adapted Confucianism to consolidate their sovereignty (Xia 65). Confucianism, like the "morals of the Zhou dynasty," emphasizes class distinctions. Rigid adherence to the social class system is legitimized and advocated. In this way, the supremacy of the emperor is validated. "Morals" in the notes are similar to these thoughts. Adding footnotes that associate the folk poem with such political ideas would not only cater to the ideological needs of the ruling class but also help to broadcast the morals among people. To some scholars, these footnotes may sound more like an over-interpretation and deliberate misunderstanding of the poems, but it is precisely footnotes like these that have enabled *The Book of Poetry* to "persist and survive in the world" throughout different dynasties and ideologies in history (Ibid. 78).

5.5   Footnotes in World Literature

5.5.1   Created Scheme and the Existing Classics: "Marginal" Cultures?

The paradoxical features of footnotes become more obvious when it comes to this age of world literature. Footnotes that include contextual information are necessary when readers reach beyond their linguistic and cultural familiarity to approach different literatures and cultures. Yet readers' exquisite curiosity about the exotic may be easily extinguished when footnotes are long and dense, bombarding the reader with too many unfamiliar messages. For scholars, conversely, informative footnotes are indispensable for anyone who is engaged in observing, comparing, and summarizing many, if not all, literatures of the world. Footnotes, within which first-hand references to different literatures or cultures are given and secondary commentaries on different literatures and cultures are quoted, are proof of scholars' competence in adopting a complete and comparative perspective in world literature studies. Through footnotes, scholars' responsible and critical scholarly attitudes are displayed. To make the information on the different and other "sheltered" in footnotes, however, seems to jeopardize the impartiality that scholars make an effort to construct in their comparisons or summations of world literatures (although sometimes the impartiality may be deliberately neglected); this means the footnotes are blamed. Such footnotes indicate the sense of superiority of the centered narrative and provoke uneasy feelings among the voices of the "periphery."

Recent years have witnessed the renaissance and ascendance of world literature. World literature enables the circulation and communication of different literatures beyond national and linguistic borders, enriching individual national literature and expanding the readership of it. Yet problems arise when it comes to questions such as how to read world literature and whether translation is reliable. Some aim criticism at the feasibility of studying world literature. Approaching questions derived from this arising field requires cross-cultural and multilingual competence, which, if possible, takes a long time to acquire. Yet given the countless literary works worldwide and the mortality of human beings, to achieve a close reading of all literary works seems to be the least probable. At the same time, the output of "distant reading" is deemed irresponsible and unrewarding scholarship either in world literature or in national literature studies. If we rely on translations, the question of faithfulness seems to be a main concern. Some emphasize the "untranslatability" and deny the readiness of cross-cultural communications. Such questions challenge the validity of world literature.

Footnotes provide a way to redress these complaints about world literature. When perspectives are necessarily macro, summarizing, and concise, which is predictably the case in world literature studies, quotations from first-hand literary works and research studies can constitute supplementary footnotes. Footnotes, either with cultural background knowledge or with linguistic help, are necessary for world literature studies. "Distant" readings can also produce a solid argument with the help of footnotes. For translations, footnotes expand the working domain of translators, as they can include necessary information or explanations without sacrificing the meaning, form, or taste of the original work. Unreasonable assimilation or unfaithful alteration in the process of translation can be avoided. Footnotes become essential to world literature in the sense that the validity of world literature can find support in the use of footnotes.

The fact that footnotes are important is not only applicable to individual literary works but also relevant to the general questions arising in this age of world literature, one of which concerns the paradoxical relationship between the universality of world literature and the diversity of national literature. The single abstract concept of world literature may tolerate and constitute the practical and diverse national literature, yet world literature may also jeopardize the multiplicity of national literature when the universality of the concept is overemphasized. When it comes to the relationship between them, there is another problem that cannot escape our notice. Should we prioritize national literature and consider it the foundation of world literature, as the former supplies the latter with abundant texts to study? Or should we regard national literature as a secondary and raw resource that is to be integrated and regulated by the refined concept of world literature?

These questions not only intrigue scholars of world literature but also entangle them into conflicting opinions. In his article "What Is World Poetry," Stephen Owen discusses a kind of "world poetry" that is completely detached from national history and traditions, and he expresses his strong disapproval of it. To garner an international audience, some poets intentionally include "universal images" that are "readily translatable" (Owen, "What Is World Poetry" 30). To Owen, such poems denote "a sense of cultural loss and decline" (Ibid.). National literature, as Owen indicates, is essential to world literature. It is national and cultural specificity that orient world literature and keep it from becoming lost in pure "uncertainty" (Ibid.). To Owen, letting national literature be overwhelmed by the overemphasized generality or universality of world literature is a tragic thing.

Another widely cited scholar of world literature, Pascal Casanova, conversely, regards world literature as an abstract but universal "world republic of letters." According to Casanova, within the invisible but irreducible "literature world," national literature is not identified by its own "textual" or "historical" traditions but is situated "on the basis of its position in world literary space," a space that features literary domination and marginalization (Casanova xii). To Casanova, what matters the most is not the specificity of national literature but its inter-relationship with the centered literature. The question of how the centered literature has exerted influence on a certain national literature should be an enduring topic of world literature, and it is the very question that enables the synthesis of different national literatures within the single system of world literature.

When William Honan describes how the footnote threatens and impedes civilization, he quotes Frank Sullivan's words: "Give footnote an inch, and it'll take a foot" (Honan). This amusing quip, however, literally comes true in Franco Moretti's article "Conjectures on World Literature." The unusual length and density of the footnotes in the article must "scare off" readers at first sight. If we roughly review the format of the whole article, we can easily find that the footnotes do not truly appear to be marginalized, as they occupy a much larger space on the pages, forcing the text into the top margins. For example, on the sixth page of the article, five footnotes in thirty-seven lines occupy more than two-thirds of the page (the length of which is not far from a foot). The text to which the footnotes are attached has only eight lines. On the seventh page, three footnotes in thirty-three lines fill the space below the text of only eleven lines. This format is replicated on five consecutive pages, from the sixth page to the tenth page, which contains only five lines of text accompanied by three footnotes that occupy forty-two lines.

So, what is it in the footnotes that is too essential to eliminate and that makes Franco Moretti, regardless of the hostile attitudes held toward scholarly footnotes, resign himself to the bizarre appearance of the footnotes in his article? Like Pascale Casanova, Franco Moretti asserts that world literature is "one and unequal" (Moretti 56). To escape from the frustrating complexity of national literature, Moretti suggests that world literature should be conceived of as an ideal and a problem. World literature is an ideal of "one literature" that transcends linguistic distinctions and geographical borders (Ibid.). It is also a problem, a problem that "ask[s] for a new critical method" that is better than "reading more texts" (Ibid. 55). The method Moretti recommends is "distant reading," which means reading "a patchwork of other people's research, without a single direct textual reading" (Ibid. 57). One of the questions to be resolved by this method concerns "a Western formal influence (usually French or English) upon other 'local materials'" (Ibid. 58). What the influence is and how it emerges are the questions to be addressed in his following arguments. To answer these questions, he cannot avoid referring to examples of "local materials" that "the Western form" has impacted. Textual evidence and a detailed analysis of these relevant "local materials" are required and expected to substantiate his argument, yet too much of it may risk the fulfillment of his words on "distant reading." This seems to be an awkward dilemma for Franco Moretti.

Thanks to footnotes, however, he avoids being trapped in the dilemma, and his resolution to apply distant reading to world literature is realized in the very article. He lists examples of "local materials" that are affected by the "Western form," and each example has one or two lines without further explanation:

> Gasperetti and Goscilo on late eighteenth-century Eastern Europe;[10] Toschi and Martí-López on early nineteenth-century Southern Europe;[11] Franco and Sommer on mid-century Latin America;[12] Frieden on the Yiddish novels of the 1860s;[13] Moosa, Said and Allen on the Arabic novels of the 1870s;[14] Evin and Parla on the Turkish novels of the same years;[15] Anderson on the Filipino Noli Me Tangere, of 1887; Zhao and Wang on turn-of-the-century Qing fiction;[16] Obiechina, Irele and Quayson on West African novels between the 1920s and the 1950s.[17] (Ibid. 59)

Moretti's strategic way of approaching problems of world literature, however, is questioned by Emily Apter in her book *Against World Literature: On the Politics of Untranslatability*. Apter's interrogation about Moretti's "distant reading" indicates her disapproval of the concept and approach to "world literature":

> Individual works of literature, aggregated in sets and organized schematically according to generic morphology, are treated as empirical entities assumed to be amenable to quantitative formalism with witty phrases and bold hypotheses about

cultural and political change, the literary Lab pamphlets adhere to the flattened diction of technics, drawing on the vocabulary of methodology, scales, frequencies, practices, principles, criteria, correlation, signals, and proofs. (Apter 55).

It seems that Apter targets her complaints at the tendency to adopt scientific methods in humanity studies, especially in world literature studies. Words such as "schematically," "quantitative," "empirical," and "lab pamphlets," which are familiar to science scholars, are borrowed to describe the methodology of world literature studies. To Apter, the trend is certainly an unpleasant one. The attempts to simplify world literature studies by mechanically following predetermined steps beginning with a "bold hypothesis" and by using the "witty phrases" that are assumed to compensate for the lack of textual evidence will sacrifice and downgrade the importance of appreciating the diversity of different literatures.

Indeed, Moretti's presentation of these examples in the text of the article resembles a lab report, as the results are simply recorded and listed. In addition, his proposal of "distant reading" is certainly bold, and his diction can be called witty, but the article is by no means lacking in textual evidence and demonstrates responsible scholarship. In fact, elaborations of how these "local materials" are influenced by the "Western form" are not removed from the article but are to be found in footnotes. The quotations and explanations are so informative and generous that each footnote, despite being in a smaller font, expands to as long as between seven and fifteen lines. For example, note 14 on Arabic novels has twelve lines, while note 16 on Qing fiction has fifteen lines, occupying almost one-third of the entire page. Both quote several national and regional scholars' descriptions of how the local fiction is influenced by Western models, with sufficient and expected reference details. As a result, the footnotes become large and dense "chunks" piled beneath the texts, which have to be typeset at the top margins of the pages. Although the layout of the pages seems strange, the unusually lengthened footnotes allow Moretti to make a solid argument using evidence from local materials without breaking his promise to keep a distance from them. In addition, when encountering the footnotes, one can easily recognize the effort that has been expended and attention that has been paid in providing them. The detailed textual quotation and analysis in the footnotes can certainly redeem "distant reading" from being called irresponsible scholarship.

The importance of footnotes as a sign of conscientious scholarship, as we have already discussed, is recognized and defended by Anne H. Stevens and Jay Williams in their article "The Footnote, in Theory." Stevens and Williams assert that footnoting "allows us a means of evaluating the level of scholarship of an essay," and they observe that "today, footnotes in a scholarly essay are not uniformly marginal, minor, or digressive" (Stevens and Williams 211). Anthony Grafton also suggests that footnotes not only prove but also persuade (Grafton, *The Footnote* 22). Stevens and Williams summarize his ideas and suggest that "we look to them [footnotes] for proof that the author has sufficiently covered the field, that enough evidence has been marshaled, that the status of the evidence has been sufficiently questioned" (Stevens and Williams 211).

Informative footnotes are indispensable for anyone who is engaged in observing, comparing, and summarizing many, if not all, literatures of the world. Footnotes, within which first-hand references to different literatures or cultures are provided and secondary commentaries about different literatures and cultures are quoted, are proof of scholars' competence in adopting a comprehensive and comparative perspective in world literature studies. Through footnotes, scholars' responsible and critical scholarly attitudes are displayed. For readers, their curiosity about the exotic may not be too exquisite to be extinguished when footnotes are long and dense. When readers face the unusually long and dense footnotes in Moretti's article, they can neither carelessly overlook the footnotes nor deliberately ignore them. They know that there must be indispensable and irreducible information in the footnotes. Intimidating as the footnotes may seem to be, readers must feel insecure if they skip the footnotes. They must realize that lingering on the few lines of the text can never help them to grasp the whole of the article. Footnotes that include contextual information are necessary when readers reach beyond their linguistic and cultural familiarity to approach different literatures and cultures.

Moretti's proposal to generalize world literature rests not on "unassailable facts" (which always result from inadequate learning or even ignorance of what is studied) but on his deep and wide exploration of many different literatures and cultures in the world. He may only choose and use references that can support his argument, but what he can choose from is determined by his knowledge of different literatures and cultures. Moretti's bold claim to distance himself from first-hand literatures and cultures is by no means an excuse for irresponsible or bogus scholarship; rather, it is grounded by his undoubted erudition and his comprehensive familiarity with different literatures and cultures. In their article "The Footnote, in Theory," Stevens and Williams suggest that "the reader goes to the footnotes to find out who is talking to whom, who is being listened to, and who is being ignored" (Ibid.). In his article, Moretti talks to scholars of "local materials," listens to their opinions regarding different literatures and cultures, and tries to present (instead of ignoring) as many examples as he can to support his argument. This is exactly Moretti's goal in distant reading: to extend "an extremely small canon" and to present more cultures and literatures on the stage of world literature (Moretti 57). Much effort must have gone into studying local materials before the conjectures on world literature were conceived. The text of the article deals with distant reading; meanwhile, the footnotes deserve close examination. The "local materials" and the footnotes are the empirical data on which Moretti's experiment to summarize world literature is based.

Yet, to distance "different and other" literatures and cultures and reduce these to footnotes in the margins (contrasted with the centered narrative in the text) inevitably arouses uneasy feelings and disagreement, especially when Moretti's own claim about the inequality of the world literature system is considered. Like Pascale Casanova when presenting a hierarchical system of world literature, he observes that in world literature "the destiny of a culture (usually a culture of the periphery, as Montserrat Iglesias Santos has specified) is altered by another culture (from the core) that 'completely ignores it'" (Ibid. 56). Local materials are compromised by the influence from the "core cultures"; they are regarded as the subordinate. Thus, it is in footnotes that the references to "different and other" cultures and literatures are to be found. Footnotes, which are conventionally assumed to be supplementary and secondary to texts, seem to be the right place to shelter local materials. Most of the footnotes are literary and cultural references to "periphery cultures," such as Chinese, African, and Eastern European literatures and cultures. "Local materials" given in the periphery footnotes are labeled as secondary. Footnotes make an unequal world literature system complete and operative in the very article that advocates it. Yet again this gesture seems to jeopardize the impartiality that scholars of world literature studies make an effort to construct in their comparisons or summations of world literatures. These footnotes indicate the sense of superiority of the centered narrative and provoke uneasy feelings among the voices of the "periphery."

The reliability of these biased subjective attitudes indicated by footnotes, as we discussed previously, is likely to be questioned. The "individual" and "personal" choices and arrangements of references in the footnotes, which suggest and support individual opinions and feelings, may not be considered as responsible or critical as intended; rather, they may be regarded as unconvincing and inconsistent. Footnotes within which personal feelings are revealed can sometimes become targets of criticism. They can be viewed as idiosyncratic prejudices or biased interpretations that are to be justifiably ignored or minimized. To some scholars, however, giving footnotes that are expressive of strong attitudes and emotions is an academic act that should be advocated. Footnotes are incorporated into the text to perform the function of stimulating and facilitating the (emotional) exchange of ideas within an essay, making the essay polemical and passionate.

We may disagree with Moretti's approach to study world literature that is proposed in the article, but we cannot deny that the article is "polemical" and "passionate." Aside from the fact that the article was published by *New Left Review*, the unusually lengthened footnotes contribute to the provocative feature of it. The footnotes are characteristic of Moretti's personal and subjective style, reflecting and implementing his idea about distant reading and the world literature system in the very article that promotes it. In addition, just as Moretti himself suggests in the article that world literature should be a "problem that asks for a new critical method" (Ibid. 55), the stimulated discussion and criticism move the study of world literature out of the paradigm of "what is world literature" to develop it into a realm of "how to study world literature." Just as Stevens and Williams suggest, the polemical article with the provocative footnotes prompts "strong thoughts and feelings." Scholars such as Emily Apter express their concern and opposing voices, drawing attention to aspects of world literature studies that should be improved. At the same time, some scholars propose alternative solutions; for example, David Damrosch, in his article "World Literature, National Contexts," suggests "national and regional specialists working in collaboration" (Damrosch, "World Literature, National Contexts" 516). That an active and lively interchange of such ideas and discussion is constantly happening within the field of world literature is certainly a positive sign for this emerging discipline, and it will nurture and energize the development of world literature studies.

5.5.2 Negotiation Between the Original Classic and the Target Audience in Translations

Footnotes are no less important to translations than they are to theoretical works in world literature studies. David Damrosch in his article "World Literature, National Contexts" suggests that "anyone involved in translating or teaching works from other cultures must always weigh how much cultural information is needed and how it should be presented" (Ibid. 521). It is always the footnotes that we turn to for knowledge about "other cultures" in translations. How to balance the original culture and the target culture in translations is an issue that has attracted enormous interest as well as enduring discussions in this age of world literature. Stephen Owen's argument in "What Is World Poetry" also concerns this question. He argues that some young Asian poets deliberately erased traces of national history in their poems, making the poems highly translatable and easily comprehensible (Owen, "What Is World Poetry" 31). It seems that they are so easy to comprehend and so readily accepted by international audiences that no linguistic or cultural barriers can hinder their circulation, nor will the translators of these poems need to add extra footnotes to their translations.

Yet, there are still poems that are quite different from such homeless poems pitied by Owen. For these poems, it is necessary to employ footnotes in their translations: They are deeply rooted in their original cultures. Translators anticipate readers' needs and provide footnotes that offer literary and cultural references. The footnotes help to clarify potential areas of confusion and facilitate target readers' understanding of the unfamiliar texts. Not only are these references necessary for understanding, but they are also beneficial to target readers who are driven by curiosity to explore exotic literatures and cultures through translated works. Therefore, to add footnotes to translations is to guarantee the preservation of the necessary and rewarding "local materials" and to protect them from being overwhelmed by the common belief in transparency in the field of translation studies.

In fact, the presence or absence of footnotes is determined as much by the poems themselves as by translators' attitudes toward the relationship between national literature and world literature in translations. Translators who are inclined to domesticate their translations must prioritize fluency and consistency, neither of which should be destroyed by reams of footnotes. Translators who prefer foreignized translations may consider it necessary to provide the target readers with footnotes that include unfamiliar information, making their reading experience of the translations interrupted and fragmented. Footnotes can therefore be essential to translations. Not only do they introduce and preserve the national literature and original culture in translations, but their presence or absence in translations also uncovers translators' attitudes toward the balance between the original culture and the target culture in translations.

David Damrosch's discussion about Arthur Waley's translation of *The Tale of Genji* in "World Literature, National Contexts" reflects such an important function performed by footnotes, and his refutation against the either-or dichotomy between the original culture and the target culture in translations is based on this reflection. When translating *The Tale of Genji*, Arthur Waley "suppressed," "delet[ed]," and "freely paraphrased and expanded" the original poem, distancing the translation from the original and assimilating it into the target culture (Damrosch, "World Literature, National Contexts" 521). But "even his assimilative translation," as Damrosch proceeds, "employed footnotes to explain the literary and cultural references that couldn't readily be folded into the text itself" (Ibid.). No matter how wildly and boldly Arthur Waley acted in altering the original poem, he failed in his attempt to completely remove all traces of the original culture. The irreducible footnotes become strong and obvious evidence for David Damrosch to rebut "an absolute disconnection from its culture of origin" in translation (Ibid.).

Yet, to some people, appending footnotes to translations will frustrate and distance the target readers and render the translations poorly received. Easy comprehensibility and high transparency of translations are what they strive for. The new poets mentioned in Stephen Owen's article "What Is World Poetry" must agree that footnotes are to be avoided. To ensure a wider circulation of their poems, they employ "circumscribed 'local color'" and "universal images" to "give the international reader an altogether safe and quick experience of another culture" (Owen, "What Is World Poetry" 28). When translated, the poems do not demand any footnotes. Such easy comprehensibility seems to have saved translators extra labor in attaching footnotes to translations, and the self-translatability of those poems seems to have guaranteed a wide circulation of the translated poems. As Owen points out, however, the truth is that such detachment from the original culture reduces the poems to "an intricate shape on a blank background without frontiers, a shape that undergoes metamorphoses" (Ibid. 32). Through the constant metamorphoses, the poems merge into the target culture and lose their origins. No footnotes are attached to the translations, nor can any identity be assigned to them or recognized in them.

Lawrence Venuti in his book *The Translator's Invisibility* describes how an overwhelming belief in transparency dominated the field of translation. To cater to this trend, translations must be readily comprehensible for the target readers. Footnotes, which complicate translations and delay the direct encounter between readers and translations, are certainly not welcome: Just as J. M. Cohen suggests, "the translator ... aims to make everything plain, though without the use of footnotes ... Little can be demanded of him (the reader) except his attention" (qtd. in Venuti 29). Venuti disagrees and points out that the overvalued transparency of translations not only renders the translators invisible but also reduces the diversity of the individual and the national to plain uniformity (Venuti 6). The effort to eliminate footnotes is taken to such extremes that what is finally acquired is only an unfortunate loss of origin. This reminds us of the "world poetry" mentioned by Stephen Owen that saves translators the effort of attaching footnotes, which always introduce national and cultural specificity into translations. Poems that are deprived of their national and cultural origins, as Owen suggests, reflect "a sense of cultural loss and decline" (Owen, "What Is World Poetry" 30).

In fact, footnotes in translations do not scare off readers as some have feared; rather, they engage more readers today. David Damrosch takes Royall Tyler's translation of *The Tale of Genji* as an example. Tyler's translation is heavily annotated with footnotes, and "many pages have six or even ten footnotes, offering a stream of cultural information that at once emphasizes the text's foreignness" (Damrosch, "World Literature, National Contexts" 522). Instead of frightening readers away or excluding them from this scholarly achievement, "the new translation has been widely reviewed in the general press, and the reviewers have specifically praised the wealth of annotation along with the eloquence of the prose" (Ibid.). It is time to move beyond the paradigm of "what's more important, original culture or target culture" to suggest a kind of reciprocal relationship between the two. Instead of being mutually exclusive, the original culture and the target culture communicate with each other within a translated work: Just as David Damrosch observes, "this either-or choice is increasingly breaking down" (Ibid. 521). The concern about "untranslatability" can thus be addressed. Footnotes help to preserve and elaborate the "whole" original. The loss and sacrifice of the original can be avoided in the process of translation.

Footnotes are informative; however, the reason why they are informative resides not so much in the supposition that they give supplementary information as in the fact that they include essential evidence to substantiate the author's ideas or arguments. In *The Waste Land*, footnotes support Eliot's argument about how to adapt tradition or the classic into new works, and Moretti uses footnotes to highlight and implement his idea about "distant reading." Footnotes are instructive: They contain criticism that not only guides readers to acquire a better understanding of the literary texts but also orients the literary works toward further and new development. In *The Waste Land*, footnotes make it possible for Eliot to shift the perspective of the narrative from the author to the critic. Through footnotes, he conveys his personal ideas and critical views of the poem, and they become a reliable reference when readers try to interpret the poem. In *The Book of Poetry,* footnotes that consist of the subjective interpretations of later scholars renew the meanings of the poems and adapt them for the emerging ideologies within new eras. Footnotes are irreducible. In *The Book of Poetry* and Moretti's article, the footnotes are too "bulky" to be overlooked. In Damrosch's discussion about translations and in Moretti's argument, the footnotes help to preserve the "local materials," which are not to be neglected or rendered less worthy in world literature. In this age of world literature, the impact of footnotes cannot be underestimated when it comes to the circulation and reception of translations, either. Footnotes are therefore no longer merely footnotes.

To world literature studies, footnotes have become essential. They are necessary in facilitating comprehensive and comparative communications beyond cultural and linguistic borders. They help to break the barrier of "untranslatability." If we borrow David Damrosch's definition of world literature as "a mode of circulation" (Damrosch, *What Is World Literature* 5), footnotes become the "foot" that smooths the path for circulations and exchanges between different cultures and literatures in this age of world literature.

Works Cited

Apter, Emily. *Against World Literature: On the Politics of Untranslatability*. London: Verso, 2014.

Aristotle. *Poetics. Introduction, Commentary, and Appendixes by D.W. Lucas*. Edited by Donald William Lucas. Oxford: The Clarendon Press, 1968.

—. *Poetics*. Edited by Stephen Halliwell, William Hamilton Fyfe, Donald Andrew Russell, and Doreen Innes. Translated by Stephen Halliwell, William Hamilton Fyfe, and Doreen Innes. Cambridge: Harvard University Press, 1995.

Barker, Francis, and Peter Hulme. "Nymphs and Reapers Heavily Vanish: The Discursive Contexts of *The Tempest*." *Alternative Shakespeares*, edited by John Drakakis. New York: Routledge, 2003, pp. 194–208.

Bei Dao. *The August Sleepwalker*. Translated by Bonnie S. McDougall. New York: New Directions Publishing, 1990.

Benstock, Shari. "At the Margin of Discourse: Footnotes in the Fictional Text." *PMLA*, vol. 98, no. 2, 1983, pp. 204–225.

Biggers, Jeff. "Who's Afraid of 'The Tempest.'" *Salon*, 14 Jan. 2012. http://www.salon.com/2012/01/13/whos_afraid_of_the_tempest/. Accessed 19 Sept. 2014.

Bloom, Harold. *The Western Canon: The Books and School of the Ages*. New York: Harcourt Brace & Company, 1994.

Bruce, Michael. "An Essay on Criticism." *Encyclopedia of the Essay*, edited by Tracy Chevalier, Routledge, 2012, pp. 267–269.

Carravetta, Peter. "The Canon(s) of World Literature." *The Routledge Companion to World Literature*, edited by Theo D'haen, David Damrosch, and Djelal Kadir. New York: Routledge, 2011, pp. 264–272.

Casanova, Pascale. *The World Republic of Letters*. Translated by M. B. Debevoise. Cambridge: Harvard University Press, 2004.

Cesaire, Aimer. *Discourse on Colonialism*. New York and London: Monthly Review Press, 1972.

149

—. *A Tempest: Based on Shakespeare's The Tempest/Adaptation for a Black Theatre*. Translated by Richard Miller. New York: Ubu Repetory Theatre Publications, 1992.

150 Chow, Rey. *Writing Diaspora: Tactics of Intervention in Contemporary Cultural Studies*. Bloomington: Indiana University Press, 1993.

Coleridge, Samuel T., and William Wordsworth. *Lyrical Ballad*. Peterborough: Broadview Press, 2008.

Damrosch, David. *What Is World Literature*. Princeton University Press, 2003.

—. "World Literature, National Contexts." *Modern Philology,* vol. 100, no. 4, 2003, pp. 512–531.

—. "World Literature in a Postcolonial, Hypercanonical Age." *Comparative Literature in an Age of Globalization*, edited by Haun Saussy. Baltimore: John Hopkins University Press, 2006, pp. 43–53.

—. "Hugo Meltzl and the Principle of 'Polyglottism.'" *The Routledge Companion to World Literature*, edited by Theo D'haen, David Damrosch, and Djelal Kadir. New York: Routledge, 2011, pp. 12–20.

Eliot, T. S. "What Is a Classic: An Address Delivered before the Virgil Society on the 16th of October 1944." London: Faber & Faber Limited, 1944.

—. "Tradition and the Individual Talent." *The Sacred Wood and Major Early Essays*. N. Chelmsford: Courier Corporation, 1998, pp. 27–33.

—. *The Sacred Wood and Major Early Essays*. N. Chelmsford: Courier Corporation, 1998.

—. *The Waste Land and Other Poems*. Edited by Frank Kermode. London: Penguin Books, 2003.

Fenellosa, Ernest, and Ezra Pound. *The Chinese Written Character as a Medium for Poetry: A Critical Edition*. Edited by Haun Saussy, Jonathan Stalling, and Lucas Klein. New York: Fordham University Press, 2008.

Foucault, Michel. "What Is an Author." *Language, Counter-memory, Practice: Selected Essays and Interviews*. New York: Cornell University Press, 1980, pp. 113–138.

Gish, Nancy K. *The Waste Land: A Poem of Memory and Desire*. Boston: Twayne Publisher, 1988.

Grafton, Anthony. "The Footnote from De Thou to Ranke." *History and Theory*, vol. 33, no. 4, 1994, pp. 53–76.

—. *The Footnote: A Curious History*. Cambridge: Harvard University Press, 1999.

Hegel, Georg Wilhelm Fredrich. *Georg Wilhelm Friedrich Hegel: The Science of Logic*. Edited by George Di Giovanni. Translated by George Di Giovanni. Cambridge: Cambridge University Press, 2010.

Hemingway, Ernest. "Ernest Hemingway-Banquet Speech." *Nobelprize.org,* 2014. www. nobelprize.org/nobel_prizes/literature/laureates/1954/hemingway-speech.html. Accessed 30 Jan. 2015.

Honan, William H. "Scholars Desert an Old Tradition in a Search for Wider Appeal." *New York Times,* 14 Aug. 1996. https://www.nytimes.com/1996/08/14/us/1-scholars-desert-an-old-tradition-in-a-search-for-wider-appeal.html. Accessed 19 Sept. 2014.

Hulme, Peter. "Stormy Weather: Misreading the Postcolonial Tempest." *Early Modern Culture: An Electronic Seminar,* issue 3, 2003. http://emc.eserver.org/1–3/hulme.html. Accessed 19 Sept. 2014.

Kellermann, Peter Felix. *Focus on Psychodrama: Therapeutic Aspects of Psychodrama.* London: Jessica Kingsley Publishers, 1992.

Liu, Hsieh. *The Literary Mind and the Carving of Dragons: A Study of Thought and Pattern in Chinese Literature. Translated with an Introduction and Notes by Vincent Yu-chung Shih.* Translated by Vincent Yu-chung Shih. New York: Columbia University Press, 1959.

Lu, Ji. *The Art of Writing: Lu Chi's Wen Fu.* Translated by Sam Hammill, Minneapolis: Milkweed Editions, 2000.

Mao, H., X. Zheng, and Y. D. Kongv (eds.). *Maoshi Zhengyi (Notes to The Book of Poetry).* Shanghai: Shanghai Guji Chuban She (Shanghai Ancient Book Press), 1990.

Mo, Yan. "Mo Yan — Nobel Lecture: Storytellers." *Nobelprize.org,* 2014. www.nobelprize. org/nobel_prizes/literature/laureates/2012/yan-lecture_en.html. Accessed 30 Jan. 2015.

Moretti, Franco. "Conjectures on World Literature." *New Left Review,* vol. 1, 2000, pp. 54–68.

Murray, Penelope. *Plato on Poetry: Ion; Republic 376e–398b9; Republic 595–608b10.* Cambridge: Cambridge University Press, 1996.

Nietzsche, Friedrich. *On the Genealogy of Morals.* Translated by Douglas Smith. New York: Oxford University Press, 1998.

—. *Nietzsche: The Birth of Tragedy and Other Writings.* Edited by Raymond Geuss and Ronald Speirs. Translated by Ronald Speirs. Cambridge: Cambridge University Press, 1999.

—. *The Birth of Tragedy.* Edited by Douglas Smith. New York: Oxford University Press, 2000.

Owen, Stephen. "What Is World Poetry?" *The New Republic,* 19 Nov. 1990, pp. 28–32.

—. *Readings in Chinese Literary Thought.* Cambridge: Harvard University Asia Center,

1992.

Pizer, John. "Johann Wolfgang Von Goethe: Origins and Relevance of Weltliteratur." *The Routledge Companion to World Literature*, edited by Theo D'haen, David Damrosch, and Djelal Kadir. New York: Routledge, 2011, pp. 3–11.

Plato. *Plato's Phaedrus. Translated with an Introduction and Commentary by R. Hackforth*. Edited by R. Hackforth. Cambridge: Cambridge University Press, 1952.

—. *The Dialogues of Plato, Including the Letters*. Edited by Edith Hamilton and Huntington Cairns. Princeton: Princeton University Press, 1963.

Poe, Edgar A. *The Complete Works of Edgar Allan Poe, VOL. IX (in ten volumes): Criticism*. New York: Cosimo, Inc., 2009.

Pope, Alexander. *Alexander Pope: Selected Poetry and Prose*. Edited by Robin Sowerby. New York: Routledge, 2002.

Qian, Zhongshu. *Tan Yi Lu (Talks about Art)*. Beijing: Zhong Hua Shu Ju, 1984.

Rosenman, Ellen Bayuk. *A Room of One's Own: Women Writers and the Politics of Creativity*. Boston: Twayne Publishers, 1995.

Schneider, Axel. *Zhenli yu lishi — Fu Sinian, Chen Yinque de shixue sixiang he minzu rentong (Truth and History — The History Thoughts and Ethnic Empathy of Fu Sinian and Chen Yinque)*. Translated by Guan Shan and Li Maohua. Beijing: Social Sciences Academic Press, 2008.

Shakespeare, William. *The Tempest*. Edited by Raffel Burton. New Haven: Yale University Press, 2006.

Stevens, Anne H., and Jay Williams. "The Footnote, in Theory." *Critical Inquiry*, vol. 32, 2006, pp. 208–225.

Stritmatter, Roger A., and Lynne Kositsky. *On the Date, Sources, and Design of Shakespeare's The Tempest*. Jefferson: McFarland, 2013.

Vaughan, Alden T., and Virginia Mason Vaughan. *Critical Essays on Shakespeare's Tempest*. Boston: G.K. Hall, 1998.

Venuti, Lawrence. *The Translator's Invisibility: A History of Translation*. 2nd ed. New York: Routledge, 1995.

Vickers, Brian. *Appropriating Shakespeare: Contemporary Critical Quarrels*. New Haven: Yale University Press, 1993.

Waley, Arthur. *Yuan Mei: Eighteenth Century Chinese Poet*. New York: Routledge, 2013.

Weinberger, Eliot. *Karmic Traces, 1993–1999*. New York: New Directions Publishing Corporation, 2000.

Whitehead, Alfred N. *Process and Reality*. 2nd ed. New York: Free Press, 1979.

Wilde, Oscar. *The Importance of Being Earnest and Related Writings*. Edited by Joseph Bristow. New York: Routledge, 1992.

—. *Oscar Wilde: The Major Works Edited with an Introduction and Notes by Isobel Murray*. New York: Oxford University Press, 2000.

—. *Collected Works of Oscar Wilde*. Hertfordshire: Wordsworth Editions, 2007.

Woolf, Virginia. *A Room of One's Own/ Three Guineas*. New York: Oxford University Press, 2015.

Wordsworth, William, et al. *Lyrical Ballads and Other Poems*. Edited by Martin Scofield. Hertfordshire: Wordsworth Editions, 2003.

Xia, Chuancai. *Shijing yanjiu shi gaiyao (Brief History of Studies about The Book of Poetry)*. Zhengzhou: Zhongzhou Shuhua She (Zhong Zhou Ancient Books Publisher), 1982.

Xu, Yuanchong. *Shijing: Hanying duizhao (The Book of Poetry: With Chinese and English translations)*. Beijing: Zhongguo Duiwai Chuban She (The Foreign Translation Press Company), 2009.

Zhang, Huaijin. *Wen Fu Yi Zhu (Interpretation and Notes to Wen Fu)*. Beijing: Beijing Chu Ban She, 1984.

Zhang, Longxi. "The 'Tao' and the 'Logos': Notes on Derrida's Critique of Logocentrism." *Critical Inquiry*, vol. 11, no. 3., 1985, pp. 385–398.

—. "The Critical Legacy of Oscar Wilde." *Critical Essays on Oscar Wilde*, edited by Regenia Gagnier. Boston: G.K. Hall, 1991, pp. 157–171.

—. *Mighty Opposites: From Dichotomies to Differences in the Comparative Study of China*. Palo Alto: Stanford University Press, 1998.

—. *Allegoresis: Reading Canonical Literature East and West*. New York: Cornell University Press, 2005.

—. "The True Face of Mount Lu: On the Significance of Perspectives and Paradigms." *History and Theory,* vol. 49, Feb. 2010, pp. 58–70.

—. "Poetics and World Literature." *Neohelicon*, Vol. 38, Jul 2011, pp. 319–327.

—. "The Poetics of World Literature." *The Routledge Companion to World Literature*, edited by Theo D'haen, David Damrosch, and Djelal Kadir, Routledge, 2012.

Zhang, Shaokang. *Zhong Guo Wen Xue Pi Ping Li Lun Jian Shi (Brief History of Chinese Literary Theory and Criticism)*. Hong Kong: Chinese University of Hong Kong Press, 2004.

Zoeren, Steven Jay Van. *Poetry and Personality: Reading, Exegesis, and Hermeneutics in Traditional China*. Redwood City: Stanford University Press, 1991.